REAPERS AND BASTARDS

REAPERS AND BASTARDS

A REAPERS MC ANTHOLOGY

JOANNA WYLDE

ISBN-13: 9781517088217

DEDICATION

For Kandace, because fuck cancer.

TABLE OF CONTENTS

AUTHOR'S NOTE: *Darcy and Boonie are characters in their late thirties during the Reapers and Silver Valley novels. Their love story started twenty years before the beginning of Silver Bastard.*

CHARMING BASTARD

CHAPTER ONE

CALLUP, IDAHO
TWENTY YEARS AGO

DARCY

"There's no room for you in here!" Erin hissed, glaring up at me from a narrow hollow between two boulders. I clenched my fist, wishing I could punch her right in the face.

This was *my* spot—she only knew about it because I'd shown it to her. In the distance I could hear the boys shouting at each other, followed by a girl's shriek. We'd been playing a weird game of hide and seek on the way home from the bus stop all week, although it seemed a little unfair that the girls always had to hide. Unfortunately there were five guys and only four of us, so they called the shots.

"You suck," I told Erin, then started up the hill again. Bitch. See if I ever saved her ass in math again.

Pushing through the trees was hard work and after a couple minutes I was panting. Not only that, between the steep hillside and the brush everywhere, I was making too much noise. Crap. I'd bet Boonie five bucks that he wouldn't be able to catch me before five p.m. I didn't actually have the money to pay up. It'd been stupid, but he'd been flipping me so much shit lately. For a couple weeks, actually.

God only knew what he'd make me do if I couldn't pay. Knowing my luck he'd make me eat another damned worm.

***

I'd first met Riley Boone when I was four years old. We moved to Callup, Idaho, after my dad blew out his back and had to go on disability. Boonie's family lived next to ours. Every afternoon he'd swagger off the school bus after kindergarten like a conquering king. For the first week he ignored me, until I'd impressed him by climbing nearly thirty feet up in the tree behind his trailer. They had to call the fire department to get me down, but it'd been worth it to see the respect in his five-year-old eyes.

He gave me a worm in honor of my accomplishment. I'd fallen in love. The next day he made me eat the worm and our relationship has been complicated ever since.

Eight years later I was still getting myself in trouble trying to impress him.

***

I was almost halfway to the ridge now, my backpack tugging me downward as I climbed. I'd been up this high before—hell, I'd explored most of the gulch over the years—but this was farther than I'd usually go this late in the afternoon. It was a bit of a risk. If I went too far I wouldn't make it home before it was time to fix dinner for my dad.

Not a good scene.

On the other hand, Boonie probably wouldn't look for me up here. He liked to think he was so sneaky and tough, but I was pretty sneaky, too.

The distant shouting faded as I clambered higher. The hillside was really steep now. The soft trickle of a stream sang to me in the distance, the light hardly filtering through the thick evergreen branches overhead. Ferns and moss and pretty little flowers grew on everything.

Unfortunately, ferns and moss and flowers aren't big enough to hide behind.

Then I saw a fallen tree and smiled. The trunk itself wasn't that big, but it'd come down sideways, lodging against several other tree trunks to form a natural shelf on the slope.

It was perfect.

Climbing up and over it, I followed the length to where it'd crashed through a little thicket. If I crawled in there I'd be completely invisible. Seconds later I was flat on my stomach, peering down the hillside from my perch and feeling smug as hell. It was four thirty already. Another half hour and I'd be the winner. About time, too, because it seemed like Boonie was always ahead me.

Not this time. Ha.

Something rattled on the slope below and I froze, eyes darting. More rattling, and I saw some branches swaying about a hundred feet off to my right. Someone was down there, but if I stayed still they wouldn't be able to see me.

Don't move. Don't breathe. Don't let him win.

Then a boot landed on the middle of my back and I screamed.

"Hey, Darce," Boonie said. "Looks like I win again."

"Shit," I groaned, dropping my forehead into the pine needles. "How did you do that?"

"I've been right behind you the whole time," he said. "When will you learn? You can't beat me."

That wasn't worth an answer so I didn't bother giving one. Instead I pushed with my hands, trying to get up but his booted foot held me down firmly.

"Jesus, Boonie. What's your problem?"

"Five bucks. Pay up."

I sighed, wondering why the hell I'd let him goad me into this. Time to 'fess up.

"I don't have the money," I admitted. Boonie didn't say anything at first, then he lifted his boot slowly, setting me free. Shit. Was he going to be a dick about this?

"Roll over," he said. I rolled over and looked at him, wishing to hell I'd never opened my stupid mouth. Boonie wasn't a guy to mess with. He got in more trouble than any of the other freshmen. Even worse, he'd started running around with some of the older kids in the trailer park ever since he'd shot up last summer. Now he was six feet tall. It occurred to me that I didn't really know him that well anymore.

We were only six months apart in age, but I was just a lowly eighth grader.

Crap.

"Can I get up?"

"Do you have five bucks?"

"No," I admitted, feeling a little sick.

Boonie dropped to his knees next to me, a knowing smirk on his face. "I knew you didn't when I made the bet."

"What do you mean?"

"You had to borrow a dollar from Erin to get a drink and there's no way you'd leave any cash at home. Your dad would take it."

Well. Looked like Boonie knew me a little too well.

I sat up and we faced each other, our faces a little closer than felt comfortable. A strange tension had come into the air. I'd known him most of my life, but these last few months he'd been more distant. Now I didn't know how to act around him or what to say.

Erin had a crush on him, said he was hot. Studying his face I could see it—he had strong features, and his short, dark hair was just shaggy enough that I wanted to touch it. Push it back, away from his face so I could see him better.

This was totally messed up—I shouldn't be thinking shit like this about Boonie. We'd always alternated between being friends and enemies.

This was different. Scary.

Boonie lifted a hand toward my hair and I flinched, feeling my cheeks heat.

"What do you want?" I whispered.

"What do you think?"

I licked my lips and his eyes followed the movement. My breath caught as he leaned forward just a little.

"You guys up there?" Erin called, her voice shrill. "Darcy! Where are you? Is Boonie with you?"

I eyed him warily. "Erin likes you."

He shrugged.

"So?"

"She's my friend."

"Come here."

"We should get going," I said, scooting back across the pine needles. My jeans caught on a branch, stopping me. Boonie leaned forward, crawling up and over my body. He wasn't touching me, but his knees straddled mine. Then his hands came down on either side of my head.

"Give me a kiss and we'll call it even."

I didn't know what to say. His eyes were dark, intense. I knew he'd kissed girls before, maybe even more than kissed. I'd even seen him coming out of Shanda Reed's trailer a few times. She was sixteen and everyone knew she slept around. Not that I judged her for it—she'd babysat me a couple of times when I was little and used to build tent forts for me. I liked her.

But I had a feeling she wasn't building forts with Boonie.

I licked my lips again, knowing I should kick him in the balls. Instead I watched as his head came closer. Then his lips brushed mine, ever so softly. Something strange and new started to uncurl deep inside. Something restless and needy. When his teeth nipped I opened my mouth with a soft sigh.

Then his tongue slipped inside.

Holy. Shit.

Erin said open-mouthed kissing was slutty. No wonder Shanda was slutty, because this was *amazing.* Boonie's body lowered over mine and I felt his weight press me back down into the pine needles.

The kiss was harder now, his tongue plunging deep into me and his fingers tangled into my hair. I couldn't think, couldn't breathe, couldn't do anything but feel as he thrust one of his strong thighs between my legs.

That's when I felt it.

Something hard, pushing against my stomach.

Was that...?

Ohmygod!

"Darcy!" Erin yelled again. She was almost on top of us and we both froze. Boonie lifted his head, staring down at me in heated silence. Whole worlds burned in his eyes and I knew things would never be the same between us again. His hips shifted once, restlessly.

"Darcy, where the hell are you?" she shouted again. I opened my mouth to reply, but before any sound could come out Boonie put a finger across my lips.

"Stay quiet. She can't see us," he whispered. His pelvis pressed down into mine and suddenly I knew exactly where this was going. Boonie might only be six months older than me, but he was years ahead of me when it came to this kind of game.

I wasn't ready. Not at all.

"I'm coming, Erin!" I shouted abruptly. Boonie's eyes narrowed, but he pushed away, letting me sit up. Then he was pulling me to my feet. Watching him warily, I reached for my backpack and slung it over my shoulder.

"I'll be right down!" I yelled, backing away.

"Stop," Boonie said.

I shook my head.

"Your hair is full of pine needles," he added quietly. "Let me fix it. Otherwise you'll catch shit."

Crap. He caught my shoulders and turned me around, fingers combing through my hair. The touch sent shivers running down my spine. I wanted to lean back into him, to feel him wrap his arms around me.

Instead I waited for him to finish then started down the hill.

"Erin, I'm headed down," I called, glancing back at him. "Wait for me and I'll be right there."

Boonie watched as I left, making no move to follow. That was different, too. We'd fought with each other as much as we'd played through the years, but more often than not it'd been us against the world—I was used to having him at my back. That boy was gone now. He'd turned into someone else. Someone hard and fierce and maybe even a little scary.

I wanted him to kiss me again. Desperately.

Erin started babbling about the eighth-grade graduation dance when I reached her, oblivious to the world-shaking events that'd taken place farther up the slope. I followed her down the hill to the road and we started walking along the gravel toward the trailer park.

"Everyone else already went home," she declared. "It took me forever to find you. What were you doing?"

I shrugged. "I didn't have five bucks. I couldn't let Boonie find me."

"Whatever," she replied, and I wondered if she'd even been listening. Probably not. She never did. That usually pissed me off but today it was exactly what I needed.

It was just after five when we slid through the ancient wooden fence surrounding Six Mile Gulch trailer park, which was missing at least half its boards. My dad would be zoned out in front of the TV with his beer and Mom was working swing shift at the grocery store. That gave me plenty of time to get dinner started on a normal night.

But as soon as we reached the central dirt driveway I realized this wasn't a normal night.

My steps faltered as I took in the clumps of anxious, upset adults. Some of them were crying. Children sat on steps, watching with wide eyes. Over at the Blackthorne place, Granny Aurora stood on the porch looking lost. I'd never seen her like that—usually she was the rock holding all of us together, always ready with a hot cookie and a cold glass of milk. My stomach sank. This was bad. Really bad. Fear and something worse hung in the air.

"What's going on?" Erin asked, her voice wavering. Shanda ran over to us, her face smeared with streaks of black mascara.

"Have you seen Boonie?" she asked breathlessly.

"He's probably right behind us," I told her, ignoring Erin's sharp look. "What happened?"

"There's a fire at the silver mine—it's bad. Real bad."

"That's impossible," I said, confused. "It's solid rock down there. What could be burning?"

"Nobody knows, but it's definitely on fire. Boonie's stepdad was underground today. So were Jim Heller, Pete Glisson, and Buck Blackthorne. We need to find Boonie and get him up there because his mom's lost her shit. Nobody knows if they got out or not."

Oh crap. Boonie's mom had gone downhill over the years. Not that his stepdad was that hot, but Candy Gilpin was a basket case on a good day. In a genuine crisis she'd be uncontrollable. Like, shooting at people uncontrollable.

"Fuck," I whispered, running across the dusty ground to my place. Tossing my backpack on the porch, I grabbed my bike and pedaled down the driveway and out onto the road. Boonie couldn't be that far behind, could he?

Two minutes later I saw him, looking more like a man than a boy as he walked toward me. My bike skidded to a stop so hard I nearly crashed.

"What the fuck?"

"The mine," I gasped. "There's a fire at the Laughing Tess. Your stepdad's underground and your mom needs you."

Boonie's face paled and I started to climb off my bike, planning to give it to him. He was already off and running. That's when I happened to glance up at the sky and I saw it.

A pillar of thick, black, oily-looking smoke was rising slowly, over the ridge.

Holy shit. What the hell had happened down there, half a mile underground in the darkness?

***

Funny how we turn disasters into dry, sterile numbers.

Three. That's how many days it took for the fire to burn out. Sixty-six. That's how many self-rescuing breathing devices failed because they hadn't been repaired or replaced on schedule. Eighty-nine men died, most within the first hour. Some were found sitting in front of open lunch boxes—that's how fast the smoke took them out.

And then there was the worst number of all. Two hundred fourteen. Two hundred and fourteen children lost their fathers that day. One of them wasn't born until months after the last funeral.

Seven days after the fire started, they pulled out two men alive. They'd sheltered under an air vent nearly a full mile below the surface, breathing shallowly and praying as tendrils of dark, poisonous smoke ebbed and flowed less than twenty feet away.

Boonie's stepdad was one of them.

The *New York Times* plastered a picture of the survivors across the front page, showing them as they stumbled out into the light for the first time. Afterward there were congressional hearings on mine safety, although according to the local union it didn't change anything. The Laughing Tess shut down for six months. Then she was up and running again, business as usual because the price of silver was rising.

None of this mattered to Boonie and me. His stepdad announced on live TV that he'd never go underground again. Then he packed up the family and they left Callup for eastern Montana.

I didn't see Riley Boone again until my junior year of high school. By then I'd been dating Farell Evans for nearly eighteen months

CHAPTER TWO

SIXTEEN YEARS AGO

DARCY

"Get your ass up here!" Erin yelled, laughing so hard I could barely understand her words. She'd already scrambled to the top of the embankment ahead of me. My boyfriend, Farell, boosted me up behind her, and I didn't miss how his fingers slipped under my jean skirt to grope my ass. Someone was horny. He'd started drinking before the graduation ceremony, although I hadn't realized how much until we were driving up the gulch toward Six Mile Cemetery for the after party. He'd nearly gone off the road twice, scaring the hell out of me.

I hated it when he got like this.

Fortunately, we made it okay and I was definitely ready to party. There were only forty-two students in the class of 1992, so they were more than happy to have us juniors along for the ride. I'd probably be here even if my boyfriend wasn't a senior. Half the high school was.

I'll never forget the first time he'd asked me out—it was one of those Cinderella moments. He was tall and strong and smart. Not only that, he played quarterback on our football team. His family had lived in the valley for a hundred years and they owned the White Baker mine. Practically royalty by Silver Valley standards.

My mom already had my wedding dress picked out, although I had my doubts. Farell would be heading to the University of Idaho in the fall and I'd seen way too many couples break up when that happened.

Fortunately, I'd only have to get through another a year before joining him. My family was broke, but I'd always worked hard in school. I wanted to get a business degree. The school counselor told me that between my grades and our family income, I'd have lots of scholarship opportunities.

I planned to make the most of them.

Popping up and over the top of the bank, I staggered to the side. Farell, Colby, and Bryce followed, then we all started across the darkened cemetery toward the party.

Six Mile had close to ten thousand graves, although you'd never guess it. Back during the gold rush, thousands of people flooded the valley. Callup might only have eight hundred residents now, but in those days we'd been the biggest city in north Idaho—home to a strange mix of miners, whores, gunfighters, and preachers. Even a bunch of nuns. You name it, they came here and when they died, they'd been buried on the steep hillside above Six Mile Creek. Now pine trees had taken over. From the road you couldn't even see the place.

I loved it here.

Peaceful graves stretched along the thickly forested hillside in every direction, covered in moss and brush.

Stone markers, wooden crosses, statues, and crudely built crypts . . . thousands of memorials for people long forgotten.

At night it turned into something else entirely.

"This place is creepy as fuck," Erin whispered with thrilled glee. She clutched my arm as the boys whooped and wandered off. I couldn't argue with that. We stumbled along the slope toward the party, which was back behind the memorial for the men who died fighting the 1910 wildfires. A terrace overlooking the grounds had been built out of smooth river stones, and was lined with benches. A rough concrete bowl sat in the center. I think once upon a time it was supposed to be a pond or something. Tonight it would be our fire pit, with the terrace itself providing the perfect place to set out the kegs.

Yeah, I know. We were horrible kids.

We were also the third generation of Callup residents to party up here, so at least we came by it honestly. Everyone in town knew where the graduation party would be, of course. Same place it'd been for the last twenty years—traditionally the cops gave a free pass on graduation night.

I stumbled on a tree root and tripped, falling into a headstone. Farell came out of nowhere to scoop me up, throwing me over his shoulder and running up the slope like I was a football. I screamed and slapped at his back.

"You're gonna kill me!" I shouted. Farell laughed and his buddies cheered us on. Then Bryce caught Erin and it turned into a race. We reached the memorial at the same time to the sound of hooting and clapping. Farell lowered me to the ground and pulled me in for a kiss, tongue shoving deep into my mouth. He tasted like beer and the taquitos we'd eaten at his house during the reception.

I liked kissing Farell. Hell, I liked more than kissing him—we'd been sleeping together since I was sixteen and he was usually in tune with my needs. He pulled away and looked down at me, grinning like an idiot.

"Fuckin' love you, Darce."

Then he let me go and swaggered off, sharing high fives with the other football players before heading over to the keg. My eyes followed him, feeling that strange sense of loneliness that always came when he turned away. Farell was a bright, shining spotlight. When he focused on me it was like staring into the sun. When he left I found myself blinking, blinded and startled by the sudden loss of warmth.

I looked away, searching for Erin. Instead I saw Riley Boone watching me with those cold black eyes of his.

He leaned back against a tree just outside the circle of firelight. People swirled all around but Boonie stood apart, studying me with a scary intensity. Like always, the sight of him reminded me of that kiss we'd shared so many years ago. We'd hardly been more than kids, but they say you never forget your first.

Gave me chills every time I thought about it.

Boonie lifted his chin in silent greeting and I nodded in return. Then someone stumbled into me, breaking the spell. Good thing, too.

Riley Boone was nothing but trouble.

***

I'd hardly recognized him when he returned to Callup. I guess his stepdad ran off with a younger woman last summer, so his mom came running home to lick her wounds. Took her less than two weeks to hook up with one of the Silver Bastards, a member of the motorcycle club here in town. Boonie's dad had been one, too, although he'd died when Boonie was just a baby.

I'd heard he was back, of course. Callup was the kind of place where everyone was up in each other's business. Still, that didn't prepare me to see him again in person.

He'd pulled up to the high school on a royal blue Harley Davidson, looking like the hero in a movie. You know, one of those teenage tragedies where the naive and foolish heroine falls in love with the gangster. Then she has to watch him get gunned down in the end, leaving her alone and pregnant because things can never work out with guys like that.

I hadn't recognized him at first. I mean, Boonie had been cute as hell when he'd left, but for all his height, he'd still been a boy. Now he was all man. Six foot three, with a bulky, muscular body and dark hair. His eyes held secrets and he still walked like a conqueror, only now he was the kind of conqueror who'd cut off your head for crossing him. Farell and his friends learned that fast, too.

Until Boonie came home, Farell had been the king of the school. Now Boonie was, even if he wasn't interested in taking on the role.

Farell hated him for that.

That was reason enough for me to avoid Boonie—Farell had an ugly temper. While I didn't think it was reasonable for him to say I couldn't talk to my old friend, I didn't want to lose my boyfriend, either. I compromised by staying friendly toward Boonie, but distant. It'd been a tense year, made more tense by the fact that no matter where I went, Boonie's eyes followed me.

I didn't know for sure, but I think he and Farell even fought a couple of times—either that or Farell was running into an awful lot of doors. I couldn't think of anyone else brave enough to take him on.

When they'd finally graduated I think half the town sighed in relief.

Now the party swirled around me in a blur of red Solo cups and cheap beer, punctuated by the occasional kiss or swat on the ass from my boyfriend. By two in the morning, I had a good buzz going. I also needed to pee. I hadn't seen Farell for a while, but that didn't mean much. I figured he was off smoking pot, which he seemed to think I didn't know about. Not that I cared—compared to the pain pills my dad popped like candy, pot was nothing. That's when I saw my old neighbor, Shanda Reed.

"When did you get here?" I shouted, running over to her. "I didn't see you at graduation."

"I couldn't make it in time," she said, laughing and pulling me into a hug. "Had a work thing."

Her words broke through the haze and I felt awkward. Shanda's "job" wasn't what I'd want, although she drove a shiny new cherry red Mustang these days.

Not my place to judge how she earned her money.

Shaking off my dark thoughts, I looked her over. "I really like your hair like that. The blonde is perfect on you."

"Thanks," she said. I wondered if she was here for Boonie, not that it was any of my business. "Damn, I need to pee. Wanna go with?"

As soon as she said it I remembered my bladder was about ready to explode. "Yeah."

"Great. You can tell me all the gossip."

I followed her back into the trees, stumbling over roots as the firelight and music faded. The night air was warm without being hot, and the sound of crickets surrounded us.

"Here, this spot looks good," she said, pointing to a clump of bushes. It was completely shielded from the party. Five minutes later we'd finished our business and headed back down the hill. About halfway back I heard a girl laughing, along with the rhythmic grunting that could only mean one thing. I bit back my own giggle, shooting a glance at Shanda. She smirked, catching my arm.

"Hold on," she whispered. "I want to see who it is."

"What?" I asked, scandalized. "No. No, we can't!"

Her wicked grin flashed. "Sure we can. They're in the open—fair game."

I shook my head, but I followed her as she crept through the darkness. Then I stepped on a branch, making a loud snapping noise. The laughter stopped.

"What was that?" a girl asked. I recognized the voice—Allie Stockwell. Well, wasn't *that* nice . . . Allie made a huge production last year about wearing her purity ring, announcing she would never sleep with a boy before she was married. Not only that, she'd done it while staring me down in the locker room pointedly. I hated the bitch.

"It's fine, baby," her partner said, the words heavily slurred.

I froze.

"Farell?" I asked, my voice unsteady. No. I'd heard wrong. Farell would never cheat on me—Farell *loved* me. I heard Allie gasp as I swayed, dizzy. This wasn't real. *It couldn't be real.*

"Who the fuck is in there?" Shanda demanded, her voice ringing out in accusation. She started forward, pushing through the weeds and I followed, praying I'd been wrong. We'd find Colby back there with Allie, or some other guy. Obviously I hadn't heard right. Too much booze.

I stepped into a clearing to find them, half naked in the moonlight. My drunken boyfriend had rolled to his back, dick flopping as he tried to pull up his pants. Allie gaped at us like a fucking goldfish.

"Farell . . . " I whispered, my world shattering around me. "Oh, shit. Why? Why did you do this?"

He tried to say something, then Shanda had my arm and was dragging me away.

This was what it felt like to be punched in the gut.

I literally lost my breath. I couldn't take in air, couldn't focus, couldn't do anything but try not to fall on my face as Shanda hauled me away from my future ex-boyfriend.

"Fuck off, asshole!" she shouted over her shoulder. "You eat shit and die."

Finally my head stopped spinning and I realized I was crying. Sobbing. We were nearly back to the party and I dug in my heels, pulling back against Shanda's grip.

"I can't go back there," I hissed. "I can't let them see me like this. Oh my God, how did this happen? Why would he do this?"

Shanda caught my shoulders, giving me a shake.

"I've got no idea why the hell he'd cheat on you," she said. "I don't care, either. Here's what I do know—if he's been fucking her, then all of his friends know about it and so do all of hers. That means everyone at the party but you and your best girls are in on this bullshit. You've got two choices here. You can run off and hide like you've done something wrong, or you can walk back down there, grab a drink, and then wait for him. When he comes back, you'll throw that drink in his face and dump his pathetic ass. Then we're going to dance and have fun and maybe get you laid by a real man, because he does *not* get to win."

I stared at her, blinking.

"I don't think I can do that," I whispered. Shanda's eyes narrowed.

"Listen to me—the world's tough for girls like us, Darce. Girls from the trailer park. They think that because we're poor, we're trash, and that's how they treat us. But we're not trash. I don't care how much money Farell has. He's the trashy one here, not you. Sometimes you just gotta cowgirl up."

She was right. I hadn't done anything wrong, so why the hell should I run away? Lifting the edge of my halter top, I wiped off my face, trying not to sniffle.

"How do I look?"

"You'll do in the dark," she said, winking at me. "Hold your head high and remember, I've got your back. Six Mile trailer park forever, baby."

***

Boonie was the first person I saw back at the party.

He leaned against a pickup truck full of massive speakers that the senior boys had hooked to car batteries. Something had gone wrong with the system early on, and it'd stopped working. Fortunately, the truck's own stereo wasn't too bad when they cranked it all the way.

Now the fire burned high and girls were all dancing. I saw Erin wander up to Boonie and lean into him. He gave her a hug then pushed her away firmly when her hands started to wander.

Shanda marched us straight over to them.

"What happened to you?" Erin asked, so drunk I could hardly understand her words.

"I caught Farell fucking Allie Stockwell," I said bitterly, wishing I could kill the hateful bitch. "Now I'm going to dump his ass."

"Holy shit."

Boonie didn't say anything, but his eyes flared with sudden intensity. Shanda looked between us, a strange smile playing at her lips. I think she was about to say something.

Then Farell stumbled out of the dark and back into the party.

"Darcy!" he shouted, lurching toward us. People turned to stare. "Darcy! Darcy, it was a mistake. Let me explain."

"Showtime," Shanda said, pushing me forward. I felt an almost palpable wave of excitement from the crowd. Great. Nothing like a little drama to make a party memorable.

"We're done, Farell," I announced before I lost my nerve. I was supposed to love him . . . but he was supposed to love *me,* too. Asshole. "Go back to Allie."

He swayed, confused shock all over his face.

"But Darcy . . . I didn't mean it."

"You heard her," Boonie said, stepping forward. Erin straightened and lurched into Shanda, clearly trying to show her support no matter how drunk she was. "You're done. Go away."

"Shut up, you fucking loser," Farell said, swaying. "She's my girl. You want her but you can't have her."

"No, I *was* your girl," I said, the words cutting through me like knives. In the firelight he looked like a homeless guy, his clothes covered in dirt and pine needles. "It's over. You made your choice."

Farell looked confused, eyes blinking. Slowly he started to sneer.

"I see how it is," he said. "You're fucking him, aren't you? I guess trash calls to trash."

Boonie growled and stepped forward, reaching for him. Farell took a drunken swing and then they were all over each other. Shanda pulled me and Erin back as the students started shouting and screaming, "Fight! Fight! Fight!"

Farell was drunk off his ass, which should've made him an easy target. And he was—for every hit he landed, Boonie got him twice. The alcohol seemed to be dulling his senses, though. I wasn't sure he even felt the pain.

He couldn't possibly last long.

Boonie was faster and more savage than I'd ever seen him. He threw a sudden flurry of punches, his face cold with fury. Then Farell went down hard and it was over. A hush fell over the crowd as Boonie turned and stalked over to me, chest still heaving. I'd never seen his eyes so wild.

"C'mon," he said. I looked around, wondering what to do. He didn't wait for me to answer, catching my hand and all but dragging me down the hillside. That's when I heard Farell shouting after us.

"Fuck you, whore! Go fuck your trashy boyfriend. He's nothing, just like you're nothing!"

Boonie stopped short, every muscle in his body rigid. Then he turned slowly to face Farell one last time.

"If you ever talk to her like that again, I'll kill you."

Nobody there could doubt him—Boonie meant every word. My former boyfriend blinked, and I saw raw terror. Then Boonie pulled on my hand again and we were off.

***

I stumbled along in shock for a while, finally realizing I had no idea where we were going, or even why I was with him, but I did know this—something monumental had just happened.

"Why did you fight with Farell?" I asked. Boonie turned, backing me into a small crypt surrounded by brush. The plaster-covered bricks hit my butt and I stared up at him, wide-eyed.

"Because he's an asshole," Boonie said. "Why the fuck did you let him stick his dick in you, Darcy?"

I gasped, shaking my head.

"I can't talk to you about this."

Boonie pushed forward into my space, reaching down to catch my waist as he lifted me to sit on the monument. Then he was standing between my bare legs, staring down into my face. A muscle in his jaw flexed. I felt one of his hands reach down and around my waist, spreading across the flat of my back. His other hand rose to cup the back of my head, fingers burrowing into my hair.

"Been thinkin' about this all year," he whispered. "I come home and my fuckin' girl is with the biggest prick in the valley. Took you too long to figure it out, babe. Such a goddamn waste."

His fuckin' girl?

I hardly had time to process his words before he jerked me into his body, wrenching my head back for his kiss. I gasped and he took the opportunity to shove his tongue into my mouth.

I thought I'd been kissed before.

I was wrong. This was nothing like what I'd experienced with Farell—nothing like the first kiss Boonie had given me, either. This was a man's kiss, his mouth taking everything from me without mercy. I felt his cock harden between my legs and God help me, but I wanted him.

Then his hips started moving in a slow, steady swivel that pressed my clit into my pelvic bone. Lightning sheets of need shot down the length of my spine.

Boonie tore his mouth away, resting his forehead against my own. His body shuddered and mine answered like we'd been made for each other.

I'd never wanted Farell this bad.

Not even close.

"Tell me no right now," he said, the words a low growl. "Otherwise we're doing this."

Reaching down, I slipped my hands under his shirt on either side of his body, sliding them along the sculpted curves of his muscles.

"I want it, too."

That was enough. Groaning, Boonie caught my mouth again, even as he shoved up my skirt. I spread for him and his fingers traced the lines of my opening through the silky fabric of my panties. Then he found my clit, creating waves of sensation and need as my body recognized his.

He teased me like that for an eternity.

Boonie still hadn't touched my skin directly but I felt the pressure building. Finally he pushed the thin fabric of my thong aside and slid one strong, roughened finger into me. Holy. Hell. I squeezed around him, unable to control myself. He ripped his mouth free to look at me. His eyes were wild and his breath came in deep, shuddering gasps.

"That's the hottest fucking pussy I've ever felt," he said, and while the words might not've been romantic, they were about the sexiest thing I'd ever heard.

"It'll feel better around your cock," I whispered, feeling a thrill of feminine power.

Boonie closed his eyes at my words, those little muscles in his jaw flexing over and over. He seemed to be fighting some sort of battle with himself. I took the opportunity to push up his shirt.

Then I leaned forward and very deliberately licked his nipple.

He exploded into action, ripping his finger out of me. He took a step back and I felt suddenly cold and alone. For an instant, I thought he was leaving.

That devastated me.

He was mine. *We belonged together.*

Then Boonie's hands found his pants, jerking his fly open, and I realized he wasn't going anywhere. He'd gone commando, and my mouth fell open as his stiffened cock burst free. It was big and hard and all too ready to fill me.

I couldn't take my eyes off it.

The sound of a condom package opening reached my ears. Boonie caught his dick in his hand, pumping it twice before smoothing the rubber down its length.

I shifted, meaning to slip off my thong. He didn't give me the chance, catching my hips and jerking them just off the edge of the tomb. I fell back on my hands. His fingers shoved the narrow strip of fabric to the side, then I felt the head of his cock pressing into my opening.

"So fuckin' good," he groaned, sliding into me with an endless stroke that stretched the limits of my capacity. Reality narrowed, every part of me utterly focused on the feel of him deep inside. I closed my eyes and let my head fall back.

Strong hands caught my hips, sliding me closer to him.

His hips started moving faster, but it wasn't quite enough. I needed more. Reaching down between us, I found my clit and started rubbing it in time with his strokes.

His cock swelled and he moaned.

"Keep doing that," he gasped. "Hottest fuckin' thing I've ever seen."

Didn't have to ask me twice. I rubbed harder, the pulsing waves of pleasure just out of reach. Boonie's hands slid down around my ass, grabbing my cheeks and squeezing them roughly. That changed his angle. Suddenly his cock was slamming into some spot deep inside that I'd never felt before.

"Oh, shit . . ." I whimpered, fingers flying against my clit. So close. *So. Fucking. Clo*—the orgasm exploded through me, my back arching as I clamped down around him. Hard. Boonie's cock thickened and pulsed as he came, grinding his hips against mine.

I opened my eyes slowly, looking overhead to see a thousand stars floating above. Reality filtered in. In the distance I heard faint music and shouting.

Boonie leaned down, kissing me soft and slow.

"Fuck, I can't believe this is happening now," he whispered. "You should've dumped his ass earlier, before I signed papers."

Stretching like a cat, I savored the ache between my legs. Who knew sex could be that good? And to think, I'd thought sleeping with Farell was nice . . . he had nothing on Boonie.

"Signed papers for what?" I whispered, wondering how long it would take him to recover. I definitely wanted to do this again. Soon.

"The Marines. I leave for San Diego the day after tomorrow. Basic training."

My breath caught.

"Why?" I asked, wondering how the thought could hurt so much. We weren't dating. I had no hold on him—hell, up until an hour ago I'd been with someone else. Someone I was supposed to love. But how could you love one guy and then sleep with another?

Boonie gave a harsh laugh.

"Because there's nothing for me in Callup," he replied, his tone bitter. "You've made that pretty fuckin' clear this year, Darce. I finally got the message. My dad was a jar-head, figured if it was good enough for him, it'll be good enough for me."

I had no idea what to say. More shouting cut the air, louder this time, and the music stopped. Shit, that was Farell. I recognized his angry, drunken ranting. A truck door slammed, and I heard the sound of wheels spinning out on gravel and the roar of an engine.

Boonie leaned his forehead against mine.

"I want you in my bed," he said. "I want—"

A sudden, horrific crashing noise filled the air, all shrieking metal and shattering glass. Boonie pulled away and I sat up, adrenaline surging.

"What was that?"

"Accident," he muttered, zipping up his pants. I heard screams in the distance. "Stay here."

Boonie took off down the hillside toward the road. I followed him, lurching through gravestones in the darkness, hoping I didn't fall and break my neck.

When I reached the embankment overlooking the road, I nearly fainted.

The pickup truck from the party—the one holding the big speakers that they'd used to haul the kegs—had rolled sideways down the bank from the cemetery driveway, crashing across the road below to land in the creek.

"Dear God . . ."

Someone was screaming in the wreckage, and I heard shouting all around. Boonie was already climbing down to the shattered vehicle.

More boys followed him, falling over their own feet as they ran.

I slid down the bank on my butt to find Boonie peering inside the cab of the upside down truck. High-pitched, horrific cries came from inside.

"Jesus Christ," Boonie shouted, looking up to find me. "Stay back, Darce. You shouldn't see this."

"Who is it?" I asked, my throat tight. He shook his head, refusing the answer. The screams turned to a pain-filled keening.

"*Who is it?!*" I shrieked. "Tell me!"

"We need an ambulance," he yelled back. "The trailer park's less than a mile away. Someone needs to get down there, make the call."

"Answer my fucking question—who is it?"

"It's Farell," he said, unreadable emotions flashing across his face. "He was driving. Allie's in there, too. It's bad, Darcy. Real bad."

***

I wasn't sure if I should go to the hospital—what are you supposed to do when the guy you just broke up with gets in an accident? Even though Farell and I weren't together any more, when Boonie asked me to come home with him, I said no. My head was too confused, a mass of emotion, guilt, and raw terror that Farell would die.

I hadn't been driving the truck, but I knew my boyfriend. Knew how he was when he got drunk. I'd humiliated him publicly and then left the party with his biggest rival—I should've seen this coming. Stopped it somehow.

Instead I'd been busy fucking Riley Boone on a grave. Jesus. What the hell was wrong with me?

Shanda offered me a ride, which I took over Boonie's protests. I couldn't look at him right now. Not that he'd done anything wrong—I just felt so guilty. What kind of girl sleeps with another guy right after breaking up with the boy she loved?

We planned to go back to the trailer park but found ourselves driving around aimlessly instead, neither of us sure what to say. Eventually I couldn't stand it anymore—I had to know if he was all right—so we drove to the hospital in Kellogg. But when we pulled up to the emergency room I wasn't sure it was the right move.

"Should I go inside?" I asked Shanda, feeling sick to my stomach. "What if he's dead?"

The thought was almost unbearable. Yes, I'd broken up with Farell—after dating him for *eighteen months.* He was my first and I'd thought he'd be my last. *Oh, God . . .*

"I'm here with you," Shanda said, reaching over to catch my hand. "We'll just check and see how they're doing."

I nodded, unfastening my seat belt. The sliding ER doors gaped obscenely as we walked in together, holding hands.

Half the high school waited in the lobby.

I saw Bryce and Erin huddled together along the wall. Both were crying. Clumps of young people I'd grown up with surrounded them, wiping their eyes.

"Bitch," someone hissed as I walked past. Shanda spun around, glaring, but everyone looked away.

"Jesus Christ, shut the fuck up," Colby said, striding toward me. Wow. Hadn't seen that coming. He caught me up in a tight hug, and I felt myself start to tremble. Finally I pulled free, and swallowed.

I had to know.

"Tell me," I said. "Are they . . .?"

Colby swallowed, his eyes red and puffy.

"Allie is gone."

The words cut through me. No. It couldn't be true.

"But she was screaming," I said, shaking my head. "She was *awake.* We all heard her. How can she be . . . dead?"

My throat choked as I whispered the word. This was too awful, too real. How had a stupid party turned into Allie dying? Suddenly I didn't care that I'd hated her, or that she'd slept with my boyfriend—we'd known each other since kindergarten, and now I'd never see her again. Not even a bitch like Allie deserved that.

And if she was dead, what about him?

"She lost consciousness in the ambulance," Colby continued. "She was bleeding inside her head. They did emergency surgery but her heart stopped on the table. They couldn't save her."

"Oh my God," I whispered. More guilt slammed through me—I'd wished her dead and now she was. I felt like I was going to throw up. Swallowing, I forced myself to ask the hardest question of all. "What about Farell?"

"He's in surgery right now," Colby said. "Nobody knows what's going on. His parents are waiting in the chapel."

He nodded toward a small door against the far wall.

"His mom's been asking for you," he added, his voice cracking.

Now I *really* needed to throw up. Renee Evans had been so incredibly good to me. When I'd first met her I expected her to hate me—after all, her golden boy had dragged home a girl from the trailer park. By valley standards I wasn't even close to good enough for him. But Renee never cared about any of that. She'd welcomed me with open arms, and eventually I spent more time at their house than my own. I hadn't let myself think about that until now—breaking up with Farell meant giving her up, too.

Pulling away from Colby, I walked over to the bathroom as fast I could without drawing even more attention. Thankfully it was clearly labeled and easy to find, because I barely made it inside before I started puking.

Everything tasted like beer and bile and betrayal.

"Darcy, is that you?" a familiar voice asked outside the stall. I stilled, clutching the toilet for support. Renee.

"I'm in here," I managed to say.

"Thank God," she said. "Are you all right?"

Better than Allie, I thought, feeling a touch hysterical.

"I don't think any of us are all right."

"Come out," Renee replied softly. "I need to see you, sweetheart."

She didn't know, I realized. She still thought me and Farell were together, that I had a right to be here. What would she say when she found out? I flushed the toilet and stood, bracing myself. Then I stepped out of the stall.

Renee looked like hell.

Her hair hadn't been combed and her clothes didn't match. Way out of character, but I guess when your son's been in an accident you don't take the time to coordinate your outfit. Her eyes were red and puffy, but she gave me a small, brave smile as she held out her arms.

I couldn't do it.

"Renee, I need to tell you something."

"I already know—or at least I know enough," she said softly. "Bryce told me about your fight. Farell had another girl with him. But I know you care about him and right now I could really use your support."

Falling into her arms, I hugged her tight and sobbed. Everything was still awful and I was confused and scared, but just being close to her I felt better than I had all night.

"How is he?" I finally managed to ask.

"He's in surgery right now," she said, rubbing my back. "They told me his spine was crushed. We're not sure exactly what that will mean in the long run, but it can't be good. I don't know what's going to happen next, Darcy. I just don't know. I'd like you to come wait with us, though. I think Farell would want that."

I shook my head—she was wrong. Farell wouldn't want that at all.

"You know, Marcus and I have been married for twenty years now," she said softly. "That's a long time—you learn after a while that you can't judge a relationship by any one thing. People make mistakes. You have to look at all of it when you judge a man. Please come with me, Darcy. Maybe you don't want to do it for Farell right now, so do it for me. You've been like my own daughter this past year. Help me get through this. Please."

I nodded slowly, because what else could I do? Taking a minute to wash my face, I followed her back to the chapel.

***

He didn't get out of surgery until nine the next morning. It was a success, in that he was still alive. We wouldn't know about brain damage until he woke up.

If he woke up.

I stayed at the hospital with Renee and her husband until late afternoon. That's when Shanda came looking for me.

"Let me take you home," she said. "You need a shower and some rest."

"Will you be all right?" I asked Renee. She nodded, her eyes heavy.

"Get some sleep," she replied softly. "I'll call you if anything changes."

Thankfully, Shanda seemed to understand that I needed quiet so she didn't pester me with questions as we drove. We pulled into the trailer park around six p.m., and I saw a motorcycle in front of my house.

Boonie.

He was waiting on the porch, his face shadowed. I got out of the car and walked over to him.

"Hey," I said.

"Hey."

We studied each other, and for once I didn't feel any kind of attraction. I didn't feel anything at all—I was hollow. Used up.

Exhausted.

"I heard about Allie," he said quietly. "Bad shit."

"Yeah," I said, my voice catching. "Farell's in rough shape, too. They don't know when he'll wake up, or whether he'll ever walk again. I guess it's pretty unlikely. It was a bad accident."

"So you were with his family . . . What does that mean?"

I shrugged, wishing I had an answer.

"I have no idea," I replied softly. "I don't know what to think about any of it. I'm just so tired . . .

"And us?"

His eyes bore through me, black as coal. I studied him, remembering how he'd felt deep inside me. It'd been good. The best I'd ever had, that was for sure. But what did having sex together really mean? He'd slept with half the senior girls this past year.

"So you're leaving tomorrow?" I asked after a long pause. He nodded.

"Yeah, I have to be at the Spokane airport by five in the morning."

"Wow."

"You need to sleep," he said finally. I blinked. He was right—I did.

"You want to come inside?" I asked. "My dad's home, but he won't care."

He probably wouldn't notice. Between the beer and the painkillers, he'd turned into a permanent lump in front of the TV. Boonie nodded, standing and reaching out his hand. I took it, then led him to my bedroom, where we collapsed together on my twin-sized bed. I'd like to say we made sweet love all night, or that we talked and it was beautiful and special.

The truth is that I passed out in his arms and didn't wake up for fourteen hours. By the time I stumbled out of bed he was gone, but I found a note. He'd promised to write to me.

I took a shower and went back to the hospital.

***

FOUR DAYS LATER

"He wants to talk to you privately," Marcus told me, his eyes weary. Farell had been in a medically induced coma since the accident to let his brain heal. They'd woken him that morning, but I'd had to work and couldn't be there. I'd come over right after finishing my shift, still wearing my uniform.

Glancing toward the ICU door, I swallowed. I felt like a giant phony, waiting at the hospital like I had a right to be here. Renee seemed to appreciate it so much, though, and even Marcus looked happy to see me.

I couldn't understand it at first. Then Shanda pointed out that I was more than someone to sit with in the waiting room. I was a living, breathing tie to their son.

It was a lot of pressure.

Now I found myself walking into Farell's room, wondering why the hell I was putting myself through this. He lay on the bed, hardly looking like himself. Between the bruises, the tubes, and the casts, he could've been an extra on a hospital drama.

His eyes opened as I sat beside him carefully.

"Darcy?" he asked in a rough, painful whisper. "Are you really here? I've been having dreams . . ."

"It's me," I said, blinking back tears. Fuck. I still cared about him—I'd come to that unwelcome realization after the second day of sitting in the hospital. Guess that's one of life's little jokes.

Feelings don't just turn off.

"I talked to Bryce earlier," he said. "I don't remember graduation at all, or the accident. Dad told me Allie Stockwell is dead"—his voice broke—"and that I was driving the car. I killed her, Darcy. I was drunk."

I cleared my throat, blinking rapidly.

"Yeah, that's what happened."

"He also told me we broke up right before it happened. I don't remember any of this."

I reached for a tissue, wiping at my eyes.

"Let's not talk about that right now."

"No," he said, and while his voice was weak, his gaze on my face was strong. "Tell me. I need to know what happened. Nobody will tell me anything. They're all trying to protect me, but I really need to know what I did."

I sighed, then nodded my head.

"We were at the party, you know that much," I started. "You'd had a lot to drink. Everyone was just hanging out and after a while I lost track of you. Finally I went into the trees with Shanda to pee. On the way back we found you and Allie having sex."

Saying the words hurt.

"When you came back, I broke up with you and left the party. Colby said you kept drinking more, then you and Allie left in Greg Krafft's truck and crashed it. Greg said he tried to stop you but you wouldn't listen."

Farell's eyes blinked rapidly, turning red.

"I'm so sorry," he whispered. "I don't know what happened, Darcy. They say I probably won't ever remember that night. I never meant to hurt Allie—I didn't even know her that well. And I can't think of any reason that I'd want to cheat on you. I love you."

The words hung heavy between us—what was he expecting from me?

"I slept with Riley Boone," I blurted out suddenly, feeling my stomach clench. "After you and I fought, we went off and had sex."

Farell's eyes widened, and I saw a flash of hurt.

"I guess I don't get to complain about that," he whispered. "Does . . . does this mean it's done between us?"

I felt a bittersweet pang. I'd loved him, or I thought I had.

But I couldn't stop thinking about Boonie, either.

"I don't know," I said finally. "Boonie left for basic training. He says he wants to stay in touch."

Farell grimaced. "Where does that leave us?"

"I don't know," I whispered. "I guess we just take things one day at a time."

"I love you, Darcy. However this works out, I want you to know that wasn't a lie. I fucked up, and I have no idea why I did it. I'll never forgive myself for what happened to Allie."

"Were you sleeping with her all along?" I asked. Farell met my gaze head on, his face anguished. The silence hung between us, punctuated only by the hum of the machines surrounding him.

"No," he said finally. "It's always been you, Darcy. You're the one I love. But right now I'm really fucking scared."

He tried to shift his arm to take my hand, a tear running down his face. Leaning over, I wrapped my fingers around his.

"They're taking good care of you," I whispered.

"It doesn't matter," he replied, his voice breaking. "The doctor said I'll probably never walk again. It's over, Darce. All of it. My whole life is over. I don't even have you anymore—I've lost everything."

His expression was so sad, so desperate. I couldn't leave him like this—so what if we weren't together anymore. I could be his friend, right? Taking a deep breath, I smiled at him.

"It's not over, Farell—I still care about you. So things have changed and that's hard, but you can't give up, okay? It's not time to give up."

He squeezed my hand.

"You promise?"

"Yeah, I promise."

***

July 20

Dear Boonie,

I'm glad to hear training is going well. Things are weird here in Callup. Everyone looks at me and whispers . . . I'd forgotten how they used to do that, before Farell and I started dating. Now they don't know what to make of the situation. Everything went crazy that night and it's still not right. Maybe it never will be.

As for me, I think about our time together a lot. I'm sort of embarrassed to write this, but I hope you know what I mean when I say I wish you were here.

One thing I need to tell you—Renee Evans asked me to come by sometimes and help out once Farell comes home. It looks like he'll be on house arrest or probation for a long time (they're still talking to the prosecutors) but the judge is a family friend, so he's probably not looking at jail time. I think they figure he already paid for what he did, since he's paralyzed (and you know how this stuff goes in the valley anyway). I heard they gave Allie's family a lot of money but nobody knows for sure. I hope you are okay.

Take care,
Darcy

***

October 1

Dear Boonie,

I hope you're feeling better now. Sucks that you got sick, but at least you still managed to graduate training. I was so disappointed you couldn't make it up to Callup on leave, tho. So far senior year isn't bad. Renee hired me to come after school and help take care of Farell, officially. Now that school started I couldn't help and still work, so this was a good solution for everyone. We got official word—he's not looking at jail time. Lots of probation, community service, all that. He's doing better now, too. Up and moving around in the wheelchair. They've been renovating the house to make everything work.

I still think about you a lot, and I'm sorry that when you tried to call the phone didn't work. They turned it off after Dad ran up the bill. Mom and Dad had a huge fight over it. I guess I'm out of luck, unless you want to call me at Farell's house. That might be kind of weird because I told him about us.

Have you found out yet whether you'll have leave at Christmas? I know you aren't real close with your mom, but I'd really like to see you.

Hang in there,
Darcy

***

January 15

Dear Boonie,

I hope your holiday was good. I feel sort of stupid saying this, but are you getting my letters? Did I do something to make you mad? Maybe I was reading too much into that night together . . . I really thought you'd stay in touch.

Now I feel stupid for even writing this. Obviously you're choosing not to reply and I know you must've had some kind of leave by now. I heard your mom's back in Montana, so maybe you went there?

I hope your Christmas was good. Mom and Dad gave me a gift card to buy some clothes, although I've got no idea where the money came from. Things are still tight here since Mom's hours were cut. I'm chipping in to pay the bills now—it takes most of what I earn.

Unless I hear from you again, I'm going to stop writing. It's been nearly three months without a letter. I still have some dignity left.

Your friend (or at least I thought I was),
Darcy

***

November 10

Dear Boonie,

I really debated about writing this, but I wanted to let you know I'm getting married. You'll probably think I'm crazy. Here's the thing—Farell has changed a lot this past year and a half. He's quieter now, and he doesn't take life for granted the same way.

Back in high school I loved him, but then he cheated on me and . . . well, you know. We both learned a lot since then, and like Renee says, you can't judge a man on just one action. Anyway, I know he'll never cheat on me again—at least, he can't cheat on me like he did with Allie. I probably shouldn't go into details, you don't want to hear them and it's embarrassing.

I guess what I'm trying to say is that what we have is different than I expected from my life, but it's good. I'm happy. I hope you can be happy for me.

And yes, I know you probably won't even read this. That's okay, because I'm not writing it for you, really. I just need to put this part of my life behind me.

Wherever you are, I hope you're happy,
Darcy

CHAPTER THREE

COEUR D'ALENE, IDAHO
ELEVEN YEARS AGO

DARCY

"You up for a walk-in?" Kelly asked, popping her head into the break room. I glanced up from my cup of noodles, hoping I didn't have one hanging off my chin. "He's hot as hell. Lori's got an opening but he asked for you by name. Said he got a referral. Wants an eighty-minute massage."

I ran the math mentally—a longer session would throw my schedule off, because theoretically it would take up two full slots . . . but that was only if I had two clients to fill them. Right now I didn't.

"Sure, I can take him," I said, wiping off my face and studying my soup mournfully. I hadn't had time to eat much, but it's not like ramen technically qualified as food anyway. "He look like a big tipper?"

She shrugged.

"He looks like a sex god and you get to touch him all over. Who cares how he tips?"

I sighed. Kelly and I might be the same age, but I felt like I was decades older than her sometimes. Of course, she still lived in her mom's basement and went dancing every weekend. She was fond of pointing out that pretty girls don't need money to party—that's what men are for. Buying drinks. Well, buying drinks and occasionally killing spiders.

These days I preferred paying my own way, thank you very much. (I could kill my own spiders, too.)

"Give me five and I'll come get him," I said. "Let me check the room first."

"Sounds good," she said with a wink. "That'll be enough time to get his number out of him. Maybe he's free to come out tonight with us? You're meeting me at ten, down at the Ironhorse. No excuses this time."

It took everything I had not to roll my eyes. Five minutes later I'd checked my room, straightened the sheets on the massage table, and turned on the built-in warmer. A small fountain bubbled happily on my supply cabinet and a candle flickered on a shelf in the corner.

Ready.

I pasted on a professional smile and walked down the hall to the reception area—then I stopped dead in my tracks. Riley Boone sat on a chair in the waiting room, one muscular leg propped up casually across his knee and a smug grin on his big stupid sexy face.

Absolutely no fucking way.

"Long time, no see," he drawled. "How's it goin', Darce? I hear you have good hands. Nice and strong, never too tired to finish . . ."

"Uh uh," I said firmly, shaking my head. "Kelly, he's all yours. I don't need this shit today."

"Oh, I think you do," he said, eyes hard. He stood up slowly and walked toward me, dominating the room. "We got unfinished business."

I swallowed, eyes darting toward the leather vest he wore. Boonie had joined the Silver Bastards motorcycle club right after he got out of the Marines. He'd never been an easygoing guy, but his time in the service made him tougher. Meaner. Mix that with his club affiliation and suddenly you had some real potential for ugliness . . .

Did Farell owe the MC money? Probably.

Shit.

"Okay, let's go," I said, my voice shaking. Once upon a time he hadn't scared me. Times change. "C'mon through. Room three."

Kelly cleared her throat nervously.

"I'll be out here. Just let me know if you need anything, Darcy. Sign says we reserve the right to refuse service." She glared at Boonie, reminding me why I loved her so much. Was Boonie hot? Absolutely. But Kelly would always put a friend ahead of a pretty face. Not that he was pretty, exactly . . . he was a little too rugged for that. Even more rugged since he'd broken his nose.

Don't pay attention to what he looks like! Been there, done that. It didn't end well, remember?

"It's all good," I told her, although I wasn't exactly confident. "He'll behave, won't you Boonie?"

He gave me a chin lift and I knew he had no intention of behaving. I had a pretty good idea why he was waiting for me today—it had nothing to do with therapeutic massage. Shit. How long would Farell's baggage weigh me down?

"Come on back," I told him. "Third room on the left."

Holding the waiting room door open, I gestured for him to walk through. I hadn't seen him for three months at least. We'd run into each other occasionally in Callup, but I'd been avoiding town since I left Farell.

My new life was here in Coeur d'Alene and I liked it that way.

Boonie stepped through the door and started down the hall. I didn't deliberately look at his ass, I swear. But as he strolled past me I couldn't help myself. His jeans hugged his heavy thighs, cradling a world class butt I'd never gotten to fully explore. Tight and muscular, not big but not flat, either. Throw in the broad shoulders and aura of control, and there wasn't a woman on earth who wouldn't spontaneously ovulate when she saw him.

Unfortunately, covering that strong, broad back of his was a leather vest with a miner's skull and the words "Silver Bastards MC," branding him as someone I should avoid at all costs.

Everyone knew the Silver Bastards were into some shady shit—I'd learned growing up that when they came to the trailer park for a "talk" with someone, it was best to go inside and pretend you hadn't seen anything. If you left them alone, they wouldn't bother you. If Boonie said we had unfinished business, that could only mean one thing.

My soon-to-be ex-husband must owe them a lot more money than I realized.

I shouldn't be surprised. He spent most of his days gambling, and not even Renee could keep making excuses after they repossessed the car. He'd been lying to them as much as he lied to me. When his folks finally cut him off—*after* I left, for the record—he'd panicked.

For the first time in his life, Farell Evans was having to take full responsibility for himself and he didn't like it one bit.

Not that I cared. I was over his shit—now I just needed to convince the club that I had nothing to offer them. Boonie had been a friend, once upon a time. Maybe I could persuade him to show me mercy?

He stepped into my tiny massage room and I followed, closing the door silently behind us. His oversized presence filled the entire space. Seeing him here was unnatural and out of place—Boonie belonged in the wild, or at the very least in the kind of establishment that could erupt into a bar fight at any time. Not in a small, dim room with a massage table and aromatherapy candles.

Best to face him straight up.

"How much does he owe?" I asked, crossing my arms. Boonie cocked his head, studying me. Silence filled the air and I swallowed. "Whatever Farell borrowed from the club, it's his problem. I moved out three months ago. We may not be divorced yet, but it's definitely over and I have nothing to do with his finances. We never even had a joint checking account and my name's not on anything."

"What makes you think I'm here to collect money?"

I snorted. "Right, you're here for a massage? Come off it, Boonie. If the club wants cash from Farell, great. Go talk to him about it. I've got nothing—I didn't even take my engagement ring when I left. He's probably pawned it by now."

Boonie shook his head, all leashed tension and predatory menace.

"I'm not here to talk to you about money. But you bring up a good point."

"What's that?" I asked. The room really felt too small. I was used to my clients lying down on the table—I liked it that way. I was in control, powerful. Boonie was way too tall, and he was definitely using up more than his fair share of the oxygen in here.

"I'd already heard you left him."

"Right . . ." I replied, confused.

"Why?"

"Because he's an asshole and I'm done eating his shit."

"What happened to taking care of him?" he asked, mocking me. "I thought that was your *job?*"

Crap. He wasn't playing fair.

"I was just a kid," I said slowly. "I thought he needed me, that he loved me. Maybe he did, in his own way, but that was a long time ago. Now all he does is drink and gamble. At this rate he'll be dead in a few years anyway, because he ignores his doctors. I guess I woke up one morning and realized I'd married my dad. Sooner or later we all have to grow up."

He studied me, those dark eyes of his impossible to read as ever.

"I had to hear about it in a bar," he said finally, his voice tight.

"What?"

"I learned you left your *husband*" —he spat, turning the word into a curse— "in a bar. Jake Preston and Chad

Gunn were talking about how much they wanted to tap your ass now that it was on the market again."

I swallowed, feeling a little sick to my stomach. Callup never changed, apparently. Good thing I lived in Coeur d'Alene now.

"That's . . . flattering," I managed to say. "But I'm not quite sure what that has to do with you being here."

Boonie gave me a tight smile that never quite reached his eyes.

"Now you're just being difficult," he said, his voice low and rough. A spark of tension raced down my spine, settling low between my legs. Thank God my arms were crossed, because I was pretty sure my nipples had gotten hard. So what if I wanted Boonie? That wasn't a big deal—so did every other woman who met him.

"I have no idea what you're talking about."

No, but you've got a fantasy, my traitorous brain whispered. Right, because that'd turned out so well last time.

"So that's really how you're gonna play it? Fine. Tell me about the massage," he said abruptly. I blinked, caught off guard.

"Well, treatment depends on what kind of issues you're having. We can do everything from deep tissue to simple relaxation." I swallowed, frowning. "Boonie, I don't think this is a good idea. If Farell doesn't owe you money then you shouldn't be in here."

"Why not?" he taunted. "Do you have a problem touching me? If that's the case, lay it out for me. How is rubbing your hands all over my body a problem for you? 'Cause it sure as fuck isn't one for me."

Hearing those words should really piss me off, because this wasn't some cheap massage parlor where women offered men happy endings. Unfortunately, hearing him talk like that was a turn on, which seemed deeply unfair.

He was the last man I should be attracted to.

I'd just gotten *out* of one shitty relationship, and while I might not see Boonie very often, I knew far too much about him. He was Callup, born and bred, and we kept track of our own whether they liked it or not. He'd given the ladies down at the Breakfast Table more than his fair share of gossip since he'd come home last year.

According to them, the man was hornier than an alley cat.

Shit. I couldn't think about that right now.

"I'm a professional, Boonie," I told him firmly. "I'll step outside and let you get ready. Undress to your comfort level and lie face down under the sheet. I'll be back in just a couple of minutes."

I stepped out of the room and shut the door, leaning back against it. Could I do this? I wasn't sure. If I'd had any idea he'd actually expected me to *touch* him I wouldn't have let him back into the room at all.

Liar.

Why hadn't he gotten fat? Or started losing his hair? Granted, twenty-three was young to start balding but that hadn't prevented it from happening to Farell. God, I wished I could go back in time. Maybe if I'd walked out of the hospital without talking to Renee that night, things would be different right now.

Except they wouldn't. Even if I'd been free, Boonie hadn't been. And now the Bastards held him tighter than any woman ever could.

"You okay?" Kelly asked, peering through the small pass-through window between the rooms and the reception area.

Say you can't do it. Just tell her you're not feeling good, you're going to throw up, anything to get out of walking back into that room.

But I'd only been working here for six months. For three of those, Farell had been leaving nasty phone messages and while Gloria had been patient, did I really want to risk causing trouble? Because getting rid of Boonie would be trouble, no question. He wouldn't just get up and walk away without a fight.

Boonie never, ever backed away from a fight.

I knocked on the door, then stepped inside. The man who'd beat up my boyfriend on graduation night (before fucking me on a stranger's grave) lay on his stomach, watching me speculatively as I came toward him. Everything about the situation was completely appropriate on the surface—the sheet covered him to the middle of his back, just like it was supposed to. He should've been just another massage client, one of hundreds I'd seen.

He wasn't, though. Not even a little bit.

I swallowed, then came to stand next to him. "Everything comfortable?"

"Yeah."

"All right. Just go ahead and relax. Let me know if the pressure's all right or if there's anywhere I should concentrate on."

Once again, the words were the same I'd used a thousand times, but somehow they seemed different today. Dirty.

Thankfully I could ease into this. Pumping my hand full of lotion, I reached down and touched his back for the first time. Oh crap . . . All these years I'd told myself I'd imagined how good his body felt. That I'd been drunk, that whatever Boonie and I had between us had been a figment of the booze and the fire and all the adrenaline that followed.

I was wrong.

His skin felt smooth and hot against my fingers, silky soft over a layer of hard muscles. My heart skipped a beat and I stilled.

"You okay?" he asked, his voice low. I swallowed.

"Fine. How's the pressure?"

The words hung between us and I bit back a giggle. What was wrong with me?

"Give me everything," he finally said. It took all I had to force my hands to keep moving. I warmed up his back with slow, steady strokes, studying his Marine Corps tattoos. Every touch reminded me of that brief, incredible night that he'd pulled me out of the party and taken me in the darkness. I still had dreams about it. Not that Boonie cared—it'd obviously meant a lot more to me than it had to him.

Not a huge surprise, I guess. We'd never even had a date. Just a fast, hard fuck. One of many in his life.

"So you're living in Coeur d'Alene now?" he asked as I started working his shoulder.

"Uh-huh," I answered, falling into the rhythm of my strokes. "I moved out three months ago. They tell me the divorce should be easy—I don't want anything from him."

The words came out sharper than I planned, and I felt his body tense.

"Did he hurt you?"

Fuck, how to answer that one? I considered my response carefully as I smoothed down the length of his arm.

"Not physically," I finally said. "But that night changed him . . ."

Boonie snorted, muscles growing tighter.

"According to your letters that was a good thing."

"You read them?"

"Yeah, I fuckin' read them."

Then why didn't you answer?

I didn't ask, moving down to his lower body instead. Reaching for the sheet, I folded it back to tuck behind his leg, fingers brushing the back of his right glute in the process. The technique called for me to fold it across, revealing the sides as I tucked it down between his legs. His muscles flexed, and he took in a harsh breath.

Oh, wow. My nipples were hard as rocks and need twisted me up into a tight knot. That strange, intense chemistry between us sure as fuck hadn't faded.

I started massaging his feet, giving myself permission to enjoy the interplay of muscle and skin as I worked him over. By the time I reached his upper thigh, we were both breathing hard. I felt a bead of sweat on my forehead, and reached up to brush it off with the back of my hand.

Despite the tension hanging in the air—or perhaps because of it?—Boonie stayed perfectly still. I was starting to actually believe this wasn't about the money Farell owed.

"Why are you really here, Boonie?" I asked him softly as I adjusted the drape, moving to the other side. He shifted, hips pressing down into the table. Without thinking, I smoothed my hand down his back. A light sheen of sweat covered it.

"Are you too warm?" I asked, moving back into professional mode. "I can turn down the heat on the table."

"That won't help," he gritted out. Okay. I dropped my hands back down, fingers trailing over his ass as I tucked the sheet between his legs. I pushed it down a little too far and brushed what could only be his erection.

We both froze, me in utter shock and horror. Men got them of course. It was a basic biological function, and I was a professional providing a therapeutic service. Like a nurse, I knew better than to take it personally.

But this was very, very personal.

Boonie pushed to his elbows, turning back to look at me.

"Either grab it right or move your fuckin' hand," he growled. "Because I'm about five seconds away from bending you over this table."

I jerked away, stepping back. We stared at each other, history hanging heavy between us.

"I think you should go," I managed to whisper. "There won't be a charge. Just leave, Boonie. I can't do this."

He gave me a slow, predatory smile. Like a shark.

"Farell owes the club twenty-five thousand. But that's nothing. He owes the Reapers, too. He spends it faster than the Evans family can bail him out. It's not gonna end well. So far I've kept them off you, babe. Let's hope it stays that way."

I swallowed at his veiled threat.

"That's unfortunate," I replied after a long pause. "But I don't see what it has to do with me. Renee gave me an allowance—it's the only cash I ever had. I have two thousand dollars saved up and that took me three years. That's all I can give you. It doesn't matter what you threaten. I can't give you money that doesn't exist."

"I don't want your money," he said, eyes burning. We stared at each other, a whole world of unspoken words between us.

"Why did you stop writing to me?" I asked him suddenly. I'd spent years wondering. Now I had nothing to lose by asking.

"Every letter you sent was full of him," Boonie replied, almost snarling. "You never said a goddamned thing about us. Then I realized there wasn't an us, at least not to you. I'm not a fuckin' masochist, Darce. You think I didn't see what was happening?"

"I felt guilty," I whispered. "You don't understand—you weren't here. Everywhere I went, people looked at me. They talked about me, called me a slut. Said it was my fault, because of our fight. Someone at that party saw us together, did you know that? I never found out who, but the whole school knew about it. You beat him up and then we fucked on a grave while Allie died. You think it was easy, walking into that school every day?"

Once the words started flowing, I found I couldn't stop them. It felt good to let it all out. The only person I'd ever talked to about it before was Shanda.

She knew exactly what it felt like to be judged.

"So long as Renee stood up for me, I could handle it," I continued, my voice rising. "And I *liked* helping her. She was good to me, Boonie. She always had been. Treated me like a family member, and it felt wonderful. Their house was clean, their food was decent, and they listened to nice music and actually talked to each other in the evenings. You were *gone*, Boonie. You have no fucking idea what I was up against. And you know what? I liked helping Farell, too. It felt good to be needed because nobody else gave a shit about me. You didn't even fucking write back!"

I practically shouted the last sentence, and my body trembled. Someone knocked at the door.

"You all right in there, Darcy?" Kelly asked, her voice hard. I held Boonie's eyes.

"Yeah," I replied. "Everything's just peachy keen."

"Okay, but I'm right here," she said, sounding skeptical. "Gloria has no problem with us asking a customer to leave if they aren't appropriate. You might want to remind Mr. Boone of that."

Boonie stared me down.

"I don't have a problem right now," he said slowly. "But if you don't finish, I will."

Asshole.

"I can do my job."

He nodded, lowering back down to the table. I pumped more lotion and started in on his thigh. This time my hands were rougher, harder. He'd said he could take whatever I gave out? Well, he was about to learn I wasn't the same weak little girl he'd known in Callup.

My hands were strong now, just like the rest of me.

Boonie grunted as my fingers dug in, finding each muscle and working it until I knew he'd be sore the next day.

"Is that too much?" I asked ten minutes later. He gave a low laugh.

"I'll take everything you have and more, Darce. You should know that by now."

After that it was a contest of wills. No matter how hard I worked him, he refused to complain.

"I'm ready for you to roll over," I said finally, feeling frustrated. "I'll hold the sheet."

"You don't want me on my back right now," he said, pushing his hips lewdly into the table. I watched the flex of his butt and thigh, his meaning all too clear.

Goddammit.

"Um, I can just do a relaxing massage on your back for the rest of the time, I guess."

"Darcy?"

"Yes?"

"I think it's time for this to end," he said, his voice strained.

"Sounds great," I replied quickly, not even pausing to gloat. "I'll step out so you can get dressed. We didn't go the full time, so I'll tell Kelly that—"

"Sit down."

It wasn't a request. *Fuck.* I reached for my small rolling stool and sat down. Boonie pushed to his elbows, putting us face to face. For the first time his face softened.

"Renee Evans came to my graduation from basic training," he said slowly. "Did you know that?"

His words stunned me.

"What?"

"She came to my graduation," he said again slowly. "Afterward she talked to me. She said that you were doing well, but that life had gotten hard for you. She told me how people were, and she told me how big a help you were to their family. Then she told me that if I cared about you at all, I'd let you go."

I swayed on the stool, trying to process what he was saying.

"Why?" I asked. "Why would she do that?"

"I think she believed it," he replied slowly. "She said she'd protect you, but only if I stopped writing. Otherwise you'd be on your own, at the mercy of that whole damned town. So I stopped writing. I couldn't be here for you and you weren't even a legal adult yet . . . She said your life would be a living hell. I knew she was right.

Every word was like a knife cutting me.

"Is that why you never came back to Callup?"

"I did come back," he replied. "The summer you finished high school. I saw you with Farell at the park. He was in his chair and you were racing each other. You were both laughing and you looked so happy together, Darcy. I had nothing to give you and he had everything. Not even I'm that big of an asshole."

I swallowed, studying his face. He was telling the truth, absolutely no question. I couldn't believe Renee had done it. Even now she was like a mother to me. Why?

To protect Farell, of course.

She'd been *his* mother first.

"That fucking sucks," I whispered.

"Were you happy with him?"

I sighed, wishing I'd never gotten out of bed that morning. It was too much. All of it.

"At first, maybe. He didn't get bad until after we'd been married for close to a year. He's got a lot of pain—the nerve damage makes it almost constant. He was drinking more and more, and he burns through pain pills like you wouldn't believe. Then he started gambling and things got ugly. His parents spent more than six hundred thousand bucks bailing him out that I know of. Like I said, they've finally cut him off."

"You never answered my question—did he hurt you?"

"He never hit me. My lawyer tells me he was verbally abusive, whatever that means. All I know is that I was dying inside. I'm not ready to be dead."

We stared at each other, then he reached out to wipe something off my cheek. A tear. I hadn't even realized I was crying.

"I want you, Darce," he said, his words more intense than anything I'd ever heard in my life. "I never stopped wanting you. Not for one day. You've been in my blood since we were kids."

Swallowing, I closed my eyes, desperate to carve out enough space to think. This was huge, all of it. Him still wanting me, learning that Renee had set me up.

That hurt. I'd trusted her.

I guess there wasn't much I wouldn't put past the Evans family. There was a reason I hadn't asked for anything in the divorce—their money didn't just come with strings.

It came with chains.

"I'm not ready for a relationship yet," I said, looking at him again. "For the first time in my life, I'm free. I'm not sure I can give that up again."

Boonie's eyes darkened.

"Give me a chance," he said softly. "That's all I'm asking."

"I'll think about it."

I spent the rest of the day obsessing about our talk. Part of me wanted to call Farell's mom and confront her—she'd been my ally, my savior, even my friend for so long now.

I couldn't believe she'd done this to me.

Of course, she probably thought she'd been doing me a favor. In her mind, I was a poor girl who'd done well for herself, marrying into one of the most prominent families in the valley. I knew better than that now.

You can't buy happiness.

By that evening I was tired of thinking, so a night partying with Kelly and her friends sounded perfect. I didn't know the girls that well, but we'd gone out a few times and they were all fun and nice. Not only that, there was a huge car show going on downtown. Thousands of people were flooding the streets to see the hot rods on parade, which meant lots of good music, cheap booze, and dancing in my future. So what if Boonie confused me? That didn't mean I shouldn't go out and have fun.

Tomorrow was soon enough to figure him out.

Popping a beer, I pulled on a short skirt and a sexy thong/bra combo I'd bought for myself to celebrate the divorce. I finished it off with a low-cut top that showed off my shoulders, and cute sandals. My hair was long and free, my makeup was just this side of slutty, and I was ready for action.

Unfortunately, it was still two hours before I was supposed to meet my friends. I decided to go down early, finding a spot on Sherman Avenue to sit on the curb and watch the cars drive by. All around me little children jumped and squealed, their parents drinking beer and arguing about whether Ford or Chevy should rule the world.

Time passed as the kids disappeared and younger people started filling the bars. It felt good to be out. Farell didn't like being around people after his accident, so it seemed like we always ended up staying home.

The Ironhorse had a live band for the night, and they'd opened up their big sliding glass doors onto the street, creating a beer garden outside. Kelly was already there when I came in, along with her friend Cherise. I knew there were more girls on the way, but they weren't going to join us until later. We did a round of shots before hitting the dance floor. By midnight I couldn't remember why the hell I'd ever considered staying home.

"I need water!" I yelled in Kelly's ear, lurching toward the bar. We had a table staked out in the back corner, but flagging down a waitress was next to impossible.

"Grab a pitcher for the table!" she replied, turning back to the dance floor. I wound my way through the crowds of people, trying not to fall on my face. I'd lost track of how many shots we'd done. More than a lot, but not *too* many. Yet. I giggled at the thought—when was the last time I went out and just let myself go?

The bar was slammed, of course. Not exactly a huge surprise, but I didn't mind waiting my turn. I could use the break. Even though I was in good shape, all that dancing left me out of breath and covered in sweat. I probably looked like hell, but that didn't matter—I wasn't here to find a man.

Fuck romance. Being single kicked ass.

I should tell that to Boonie, I decided. He might be hot and have a nice dick, but I wasn't going to let any man tie me down. *Ha!*

"Can I buy you a drink?" asked a guy next to me, and I turned to look at him. He was cute—probably around my age or a little older, with a shock of dark black hair and green eyes. He was all frat boy, coated in a thick layer of Abercrombie and Fitch. Kelly would be all over him.

I opened my mouth to tell him I was married, then snapped it shut again *because I wasn't married anymore!*

Holy *crap,* that was awesome. Suddenly I grinned at him like an idiot, leaning toward him to say, "No, but thanks for asking."

I turned away to find the bartender smirking at our little exchange, and shrugged my shoulders in a "whatcha gonna do?" kind of move.

"Can I get a pitcher of water?"

"And a round of kamikazes," a deep voice said behind me. I froze as big arms reached down to grasp the bar on either side of me.

Boonie?

I could see his reflection in the mirror behind the bartender. He stepped closer, crowding and covering me with his powerful body. Then he leaned down, smoothing aside my hair to speak directly in my ear.

"That guy sitting next to you looks like he wants to eat you," he said. "You give him anything that should be mine?"

I stiffened, refusing to reply as the bartender set a tray of shots in front of us. Then I reached into a pocket to pay for them, because like I said—I buy my own drinks.

Boonie wrapped an arm around my waist, trapping my hand as he handed the bartender a wad of bills.

"I ordered the fuckin' shots," he rumbled in my ear. "What's got your panties in a knot?"

I smelled alcohol on his breath and I wondered who he'd been drinking with. Was it a woman? I turned in his arms to frown at him.

"I've decided to stay single for the rest of my life," I announced grandly. "I don't care how good you are at sex—I'm not interested."

Boonie gave a shit-eating grin as he tipped the bartender.

"So you think I'm good at sex?"

"Don't be a dumbass," I said, rolling my eyes. Uh oh. That made me dizzy. I caught his arm and steadied myself, wondering what I'd been planning to say.

"Where's your table?" he asked. I glared at him.

"It's full," I declared. "We don't have room for you."

"You can sit on my lap."

He wasn't kidding about sitting on his lap. Kelly and the others squealed with excitement when they saw the tray of kamikazes, and they squealed harder when five big men wearing Silver Bastard and Reapers MC colors came to join us.

"You know," Kelly slurred, leaning toward Boonie. "I didn't like you very much this afternoon—even wished I hadn't told you where to find us. I'm really glad I did."

I turned on her.

"You're responsible for this?" I demanded. "I thought you were on my team!"

"I'm sorry! It was before you took him back with you—remember I said I was trying for his phone number? And he bought us shots. He's a good guy."

I frowned, not liking how he'd pumped my friend for information. In all fairness, though, she'd probably been the one doing the pumping.

Pumping. Ha. A fit of giggles overtook me as I reached for another tiny glass.

"What's so funny?" Boonie asked, his lips tracing the edges of my ear. It distracted me long enough for him to take away my drink and set it out of reach, which was really unfair. Then his hand started running up and down my thigh under the table and I forgot all about the booze.

"Kelly pumped you," I said, giggling again.

He gave a low laugh. "Darce, you're hot as hell but I got no fuckin' idea what you're talking about."

I let my head flop back on his shoulder, smiling at him. God, he was beautiful. Kelly squawked as one of the bikers caught her hand, dragging her off toward the dance floor.

"You want to dance?" Boonie asked. I nodded, grinning at him. "I take it that means you're over your snit?"

I frowned. "What snit?"

"At the bar. You looked pissed to see me. I wondered what'd been going through that brain of yours."

I frowned, trying to remember. Oh, yeah. I wasn't married anymore. That was pretty fabulous.

"I like being single," I informed him. "I like how nobody tells me what to do. If you tell me what to do, that'll piss me off."

He laughed, then leaned close.

"Babe, I'm not Farell."

I shifted in his lap, feeling the bulge of his cock flex under my ass. A wave of heated need ran through me, and my drunken mouth spoke before giving my brain a chance to weigh in.

"The last time I had any real penis/vagina action was with you in that cemetery," I said, trying to focus on his face. Unfortunately things had started to spin, making it damned hard. Ha. *Hard.* I liked hard things. "Farell couldn't get it up after the accident. We still fooled around and he got me off, but even that hasn't happened for at least a year."

"Jesus Christ," he groaned, turning me toward him. One hand caught my hair, and then he was kissing me, tongue diving deep into my mouth. His dick turned rock solid under my ass and I wiggled happily because everything was tingly between my legs—*woohoo!*

The night turned fuzzy after that.

I know we danced for a long time. We also made out a bunch, which was perfectly fine because after every kiss I reminded him that I absolutely, positively wasn't interested in a relationship.

Boonie just nodded and smiled—then he'd kiss me again.

The only part that wasn't so great were the other bikers. Now that I knew how much money Farell owed, I was a little scared they might ask me about it. Fortunately, they were too busy trying to convince Kelly and the others to come back to their clubhouse and party to pay attention to me.

By last call, I was exhausted, starving, and horny as hell.

That's when Kelly stood and informed us we needed a "potty break." We all trouped to the bathroom in a giggly, wobbling clump, taking turns using the disgusting little stall as Kelly called for a vote.

"So what's next, girls? We going to that party or doing our own thing?"

I frowned into the mirror, then made fish lips at myself. *Glub. Glub.* Funny . . . Sudden, loud shouting broke through my alcoholic fog and I blinked. This wasn't happy, "We're at the bar!" shouting. These were definitely "Holy shit, something's really wrong!" sounds.

"What the fuck?" Kelly asked as we looked at each other with wide eyes. Creeping to the door, I opened it a smidge. People were rushing through the hall toward the emergency exit. Not good.

"We gotta get out of here," I told her. Someone pushed against the door and I stepped back as Boonie opened it, his face dead serious.

"C'mon, all of you," he said, grabbing my wrist to pull me out into the hall. The rest of the girls followed and then his friends were with us as we joined the tide of people. I still had no idea what the hell was going on. After a few long, confusing minutes the flow of bodies burst out into the alley and I saw flashing lights everywhere.

"Fuck," Boonie said, jerking me closer. Good thing, too, because people were lurching and falling all around us. I heard someone shouting over a loudspeaker, but I couldn't tell what they were saying.

We started following the back of the building, trying to get away from the crowd. In the distance I heard more cries and screams. I couldn't see Kelly anymore. I couldn't really see anything—just random people rushing in all directions, their faces panicked.

After an eternity of waiting, we reached the end of the alley and ran into the street. That's when I saw the line of cops wearing riot gear and carrying plastic shields. They were shouting something . . .

"Get back!"

"Oh, fuck," Boonie muttered. Suddenly a rock flew over our heads. It hit one of the cops. Then a glass beer bottle shattered against a shield. The police line faltered, and one of them stepped out of line, lifting his baton to hit a man who'd been standing too close. Suddenly the others started hitting people, too, and the crowd panicked. Everyone surged back but there was nowhere to run—the wall of people behind us just kept pressing forward. I felt Boonie's grip on me slip.

"Boonie!" a man yelled. I looked over to see one of his biker friends waving at us. He plowed into the crowd, cutting a line toward us. Boonie caught me up, throwing me over his shoulder as he moved toward his friend. People were throwing more rocks now as the police kept fighting them.

What the hell? *Things like this don't happen in Coeur d'Alene!*

The crowd ebbed and surged around us as Boonie fought free, then we were running across Lakeside Avenue into the neighborhood just north of downtown. We weren't the only ones fleeing—all around people ran up the street, screaming and crying. I'd never seen anything like it.

"You okay?" Boonie asked, setting me back down. I nodded.

"The others already left," his friend said.

"Thanks, brother," Boonie told him. I looked at the biker, noting the Silver Bastard patches he wore. This man had thrown himself into a rioting crowd to guide us to safety, I realized. No wonder Boonie considered him a brother. For the first time, I realized the club might be more than a criminal gang . . .

"Thank you," I said, and the man offered a toothy smile. I saw a trail of blood trickling down his forehead.

"Are you hurt?"

"No worries," he said, wiping at it. "One of 'em got me, but I got him back."

The sudden, bright light of a spotlight filled my eyes.

"Stay where you are," a voice said over a loudspeaker.

"Let's go!" Boonie's friend shouted, then we were running again as the sound of the rioting crowd grew louder behind us.

***

Ten minutes later, Boonie and I slowed to a walk as we moved up Fifth Street. I had no idea where his friend had gone, or where Kelly was.

"Would your friends have taken the girls with them?" I asked Boonie as we stopped to lean against a wooden privacy fence. My breath came hard and my side hurt from running. At least I wasn't feeling drunk anymore. Way too much adrenaline…

"Yeah, they should be fine," he said, rubbing the back of his neck. "We planned it out when we came looking for you. Fuck. Don't take this the wrong way, but every time I kiss you something blows up. I'm startin' to think we're cursed."

I looked at him, and realized he was right. First the mine, then Farell's crash . . . now whatever the ever-loving hell this had been.

"Damn. What do you think would happen if we actually made it to a second date?"

He stared at me, then his face cracked and he started laughing. I caught his mood, and then we were both laughing so hard tears ran down my face.

"Fuck if I know," he said admitted finally. "Apocalypse or some shit?"

I sobered, frowning at him. He was joking, of course, but he raised a point. Bad things really did seem to happen every time we got together.

"Maybe for the good of humanity we should call it quits?"

"No way," he said, pulling me into his body for a hard kiss. My insides heated and I guess I wasn't totally sober after all, because I felt absolutely no inhibitions.

A car sped by and someone shouted, "Cops are coming!"

Boonie dropped me abruptly. Down the street I saw the flash of blue lights.

"Are you kiddin' me?" he asked, glancing around. "Over here."

I followed him into the alley behind the fence. The yard had a gate, but it was locked. Not a problem for Boonie—he caught the edge of the fence and jumped, boosting himself up and over. Seconds later the gate opened from the inside. I ran through right before the squad car turned down the alley. Boonie slammed it shut behind me, and we both leaned back against it, panting.

"Are they looking for us?" I asked, confused.

"Doubt it," he replied. "I mean, they always target the club, but I'm thinkin' they just want to clear out downtown."

"What the hell happened? Did you see anything?"

"Yeah," he said. "There was a biker outside the bar. The cops were givin' him shit, and then some guys in the crowd started arguing with them. By the time I realized what was happening, the biker was already gone. Still not quite sure how it turned into a riot."

I glanced at him sharply. "Was he one of your friends?"

"Nope. Never saw him before and he wasn't wearing club colors. All happened pretty damned fast. I think the cops panicked."

Beyond the fence more lights flashed. We heard the police car pull into the alley, then it stopped and the lights went dark. I heard the crackle of the cop's radio—he'd parked there. Crap.

"So now what?" I whispered. "I think we're stuck here."

Boonie shook his head, lifting a finger to his lips but it was too late.

"You hear something?" a voice asked. Suddenly a flashlight hit the other side of the fence, narrow strips of light shining through the cracks in the boards. I gasped. In an instant, Boonie caught me, covering my mouth with his hand.

"Boost me up," said another man. "I'll look over the top, maybe I'll see something."

Boonie let my mouth go, holding my gaze intently. As the cops shifted just inches from us, he jerked his chin behind me. I glanced around to see an overgrown lilac shrub—it was more than big enough to hide us . . . assuming we could reach it.

Fortunately we'd been in this situation before.

Not with the cops, of course. But when we'd been kids we'd had a far more terrifying nemesis.

Granny Blackthorne.

Twice a week she baked bread for her family, which she'd set out on her back porch. She also put out cookies, cupcakes, and even the occasional pie.

Looking back, it's obvious that she was leaving the food for the kids in the trailer park. Most of us had enough to eat—at least during the school year, when we could get free lunches at school—but a lot of it was cheap, prepackaged shit. Not long after the worm incident, Boonie had judged me worthy to join his raiding party. Because I'd been a cute little girl, they'd used me as bait. I'd pick a handful of wildflowers, then go knock at Granny's door. After a few minutes—her hearing wasn't so good—she'd answer and I'd hold them out, offering my best gap-toothed smile and lisping about how much I liked her roses.

It was my job to keep her talking as long as possible, while Boonie and the boys went raiding. I'd wait for the signal and then run off to get my share of the booty.

She never caught on to us—or so we assumed—but no matter how much we stole, she put out more. Along the way, we'd developed a whole secret language of elaborate hand gestures, winks, et cetera, because you never knew what might happen during a highly dangerous food raid.

Now Boonie blinked at me twice in the old pattern.

Back up.

The cops were talking again, then I heard a flashlight hitting the boards. I nodded understanding, taking two steps backward as Boonie guided me. He caught my hands and lowered me to the ground. Seconds later I'd scooted silently into the safety of the shrub. Boonie followed, crawling over my body just in time.

Behind him—through the leaves—I saw the cop peering over the fence, shining his light into the back yard. Boonie looked down on me, his body heavy as we lay perfectly still.

"You see anything?" the cop asked his partner.

"Nope, looks clear."

The man grunted as he dropped back down, his radio crackling again. I became more aware of Boonie's weight pinning me in the darkness. His legs tangled with mine, reminding me of that afternoon in the woods above the trailer park.

He'd been heavy on me then, too. Now his hips pressed down and his mouth dropped over mine.

I wanted to protest—the cops were less than five feet away—but he didn't give me a chance. He nipped at my lip, then shoved his tongue deep inside as I gasped. My head started to spin as he kissed me, taking advantage of the fact that I couldn't risk making a sound.

When his hand trailed down my side, sliding between us to catch my thigh, I started getting nervous. When he pushed my leg out to grind his pelvis into me I felt something like panic, knowing there wasn't much Boonie wouldn't dare.

How far would he take this?

Farther than was comfortable. His cock pushed into the softness between my legs and like always, the chemistry between us was instant and powerful. He shifted, his erection rubbing against my clit. For long minutes he swiveled his hips slowly, pressing me back into the dirt as fire raced up my spine.

I wanted to strain against him but I couldn't—he was already being so reckless, so crazy. No matter what I did, I'd risk making noise. Not that they had any reason to arrest us.

Not any legitimate reason.

But not half an hour ago I'd watched the police beating people with clubs, people just like me—and that was in front of *witnesses.* What would they do here in the dark, where nobody could see them?

Boonie pushed up on one arm, still holding my lips captive as he reached down to catch my shirt. Then his fingers caught my left nipple, pinching it lightly and tugging as his hips kept their steady rhythm.

We heard thudding footsteps as a group of people ran by, the police parked beyond the fence racing to meet them. Someone screamed. I couldn't move, couldn't think, couldn't do anything.

Boonie wasn't so inhibited.

Taking advantage of the distraction, he lifted his hips and reached down to unzip his pants. Then he pulled up my skirt and I felt my ass hit the bare dirt.

I really needed to stop wearing skirts.

Seconds later his fingers slid inside me and I'm embarrassed to admit how wet I was already. (Okay, make that stop wearing skirts and invest in some serious granny panties, because these thongs weren't providing any protection at all.)

His thumb found my clit as his fingers hit my g-spot. I arched my back, and I would've cried out if he hadn't caught my mouth with his again, swallowing the sound.

Overhead lights flashed and outside the fence people shouted. I hardly even noticed, because Boonie pulled out and grabbed his cock, lining it up with my entrance.

Then he pushed inside.

Looking back, it's hard to keep all of it straight. I know the chaos around us seemed to be moving away, but I could still hear the police radio on the other side of the fence. Boonie's strokes were steady and smooth, not to mention so achingly slow that they were torture. I pushed my hands down into his jeans and cupped his ass, urging him to go faster. He ignored me, maintaining his pace as more people ran by. The chemistry between us had always been insane, but this time it was explosive and by the time I came, he had to cover my mouth with his hand to keep me silent. At the last minute he pulled out, blowing his wad on my stomach as the fireworks were still exploding in my head.

Then he shifted, rolling us to our sides and tugging me onto his body, rubbing one hand through my hair as the noises around us faded. It was just me and him, joined in our own private world.

You'd think the adrenaline would've kept me up all night, but apparently it wasn't enough to overpower the sex and the booze. At some point I drifted off, despite the lights and the noise.

Boonie woke me with a kiss, raising one knee up between my legs as I squirmed against him restlessly.

Then a branch poked my ass and I remembered where we were.

"What the hell was that all about?" I asked, my voice a soft whisper.

"I think it was a riot. Although I still can't quite figure out how it started. Never heard of one around here before."

I shivered, and he tightened his arms around me, rubbing up and down my back.

"That's pretty fucked up."

"No shit," he said, then distracted me with another kiss. I pushed back against his leg, realizing my skirt was still up around my waist.

Slutty, much?

"Um . . . I'm not sure—" I started to say, but he cut me off.

"Don't think about it too much. Not gonna end well for either of us. Just consider this—every time we've gotten together, some big disaster hits. This time it missed us. Maybe that means we're home free."

I frowned at him, flinching as pain shot through my skull.

"Hangover?" he asked. I nodded. "You need some coffee and some food."

"And a shower."

"Great," he said. "We've got all of that at my friend's place. It's not far—will take us about ten minutes to walk there."

There are walks of shame, and Walks of Shame. I think when you come dragging in after a riot, covered in dirt, leaves, and dried come, you qualify for capital letters by default. We saw a few police cars along the way, but things seemed to be settling down. Early light traced the sky. If I hadn't known better, I'd never have guessed there'd been people fighting in the streets just hours before.

His friend's place was just an apartment over a garage. When we walked in, the first thing I saw was Kelly asleep on the couch. Well, she was on top of a man on the couch—the same man who'd helped rescue us from the crowd.

He opened his eyes briefly, then closed them again. More people slept in the bedroom, but at least the bathroom was empty. I followed Boonie through the wooden door, then frowned when he reached for his leather cut.

"Maybe we should shower separately?"

He shook his head.

"No way. Took me long enough to pin you down. I let you out of my sight you might go marry someone else."

I think he meant it as a joke, but I frowned.

"Boonie, I was serious when I said I wasn't ready for a relationship. The divorce isn't even final yet—I can't handle anything new."

He pulled off his leather, hanging it carefully on a hook. Then he reached for the edges of his shirt.

"I get that," he said, tugging it over his head. The sight of his bare chest caught me. Damn, this man was beautiful . . . "But what we have between us isn't new, Darce. It's always been here. I had to walk away twice. I won't do it again."

He was right. There really had always been something between us, and not just when it came to sex. As children he'd always protected me . . . well, protected me from everyone but himself. He'd fought Farell for me, and even when he'd stopped returning my letters, he'd thought he was doing it for my benefit.

This wasn't new at all.

"I'm not willing to give up what I have," I insisted, refusing to roll over. I'd had my fill of that with Farell. "My whole life I've had to live for other people. This is my time. I'm not willing to let that go, not even for you."

"Does having 'your time' involve you fucking guys who aren't me?"

I rubbed my stomach, a thrill running through me at the memory or him, deep inside. Could I imagine doing that with someone else?

Not really.

"No, but it doesn't involve me moving back to Callup and giving up my career, either. I want to own my own spa some day—one of those places where people come to get their hair done, along with manicures and massages and all that."

"Sounds great, so long as I don't have to get my nails painted," he said, shrugging. "But I definitely want more of those massages. Wouldn't mind a happy ending, either."

"Not funny," I snapped. "I'm a therapist, Boonie. I help people who are in pain. You should respect that."

The smiled dropped from his face and he caught my hands, pulling me close.

"It was just a joke, Darce," he said. "I don't need you giving up on your dreams. Hell, I've got my own life. The last thing I want is you all whiny and dependent. My mom was like that. Sucked. I just want to know that at the end of the day you'll be in my bed."

I leaned into him, laying my head on his chest.

"I could probably make that work. But no more riots, okay? My ass is covered in scratches. Let's keep it boring from now on."

"Boring. I can work with that."

A sudden knocking pounded the door.

"Boonie, get out here!" his friend shouted. "You won't believe what just happened."

Boonie pulled away, running a hand through his hair in frustration.

"I think we're going to have to be bored later," he muttered. I sighed, realizing I should probably get used to it.

"We really are cursed."

Boonie shook his head, then gave my nose a quick kiss.

"We're just normality-challenged. It'll be okay."

Wrapping my arms around him, I gave a squeeze then let him go. Guess I should get used to it—boring was probably overrated anyway, right?

* * *

Historical note: The events in this story are based loosely on real events that took place at different times in the Silver Valley and Coeur d'Alene, Idaho.

The "riot" in downtown Coeur d'Alene took place in June 1999, during the annual Car d'Alene classic car show. It began outside the Ironhorse Saloon when police stopped a biker and were booed by the crowd. Things grew out of control when more officers arrived in riot gear. While the exact timeline of events is controversial, many witnesses (including my own friends who were present) stated that the police attacked them violently. Fourteen people were arrested and it led to a challenge in the Idaho State Supreme Court over whether police officers are immune from prosecution.

The Sunshine Mine Fire is one of the darkest chapters in Silver Valley history. On May 9, 1972, the second deadliest hard-rock mining disaster in U.S. history killed ninety-one men deep underground, many of whom were overcome so quickly they were found still sitting in front of their open lunch boxes. Escape efforts were hampered by out-of-date rescue equipment and leadership issues. Eight days later, two survivors were found 4,800 feet under the surface. No other men would come out alive. The oldest victim was sixty-one years old and the youngest was nineteen. They left behind seventy-seven widows and more than two hundred children, three of whom were still unborn. If you're interested in learning more, I highly recommend *The Deep Dark* by Gregg Olsen.

AUTHOR'S NOTE: *This is one of the first scenes from* Reaper's Property, *told from an alternative point of view. It is appropriate for readers who haven't already read the book, and was originally published on my website.*

STICKY SWEET

HORSE

"I'm so sick of this shit."

I pulled the nozzle out of my bike's gas tank and wiped off my forehead, rubbing my hand dry against my faded jeans. My black leather vest concentrated the heat on my back, and the thought of cramming my head back into my oven of a helmet pissed me off. It'd been a long, hot ride, and the weather in this shithole of a town wasn't helping my mood. "Fuckin' excuses, every time I talk to him."

"Yeah," Picnic said, glancing toward the convenience store behind the pumps. Max was inside grabbing something to drink. "I hear you. You think Jensen will admit he fucked up or keep up the lies?"

I glanced at him and shrugged, sick of the situation. Why had the Reapers gotten into business with Jeff Jensen, anyway? The guy might be a genius when it came to getting money out of the country, but he was still a fuckin' stoner. Couldn't trust them for shit.

No follow-through.

"He doesn't have a good reason for this latest mess, then I'm about done with the asshole," I muttered, running the numbers through my head. Jeff had made our motorcycle club a shitload of money, but the constant babysitting . . . I wasn't sure it was worth it anymore. Should've kicked him out on his ass when he first came to us with his little business proposal. "Goddamn, it's hot out here. Why the fuck would anyone choose to live in eastern Washington, anyway?"

Picnic raised a brow.

"I thought he was some kind of idiot savant, a 'valuable asset'?" he asked lightly. "You told us all about it yesterday. What's the matter, sun got you all grumpy? You need a cool bath, maybe a Midol to soothe your temper, sweetheart?"

I narrowed my eyes at my club president, then felt a rueful grin tugging at my lips. Pic was right. Reapers didn't whine like little bitches—I needed to grab sack and deal.

"You're a dick," I said. Picnic grinned back at me.

"Ya think?"

"Hey, you ladies ready?" Max yelled, walking out of the store. He stopped next to the bikes, handing over bottles of cold water. "Or do we need some more time to discuss the issue? Because I'm sick of talking about this guy. We should teach him not to fuck with us, so we don't have to keep making trips like this."

I ignored Max, dropping my head to one side, stretching out my neck. I wondered if we'd made the right call, bringing a third man along. Max had volunteered, but he had a short temper, and Jensen needed careful management. On the other hand, maybe he was right—a good scare might catch the little fucker's attention, help him focus.

"Let's go," Pic said. I swung a leg over my bike and kicked it to life. Might as well get it over with.

As we rolled down the long, tree-lined driveway toward Jensen's little shack, I saw an unfamiliar car parked outside. Not Jeff's Firebird, but some little plastic hatchback thingie. I glanced over at the trailer, seeing a picnic table in the yard. A chick sat up slowly on top of it.

A fuckin' hot chick.

Trip might not be a total suckfest after all.

The woman watched as we pulled up with a roar, her eyes wide, long dark hair tangled around her face, and tits all but popping out of the microscopic red bikini top she wore. She was small, smaller than my usual type, but she had all the right curves. Her legs were spread, her cutoffs were short and they gaped enough that I could tell she wore something red underneath. The rest of the bikini? Matching panties? G-string? Now that would be real nice . . .

My dick sat up and suggested we investigate.

I'd never been one to ignore my dick.

Glancing over at Pic, I jerked my head toward the girl, silently claiming her. Pic smirked at me, but he shrugged, agreeing. I didn't bother looking at Max. Brother might want in on the action, but he was still probationary, so he could wait the fuck in line for the next available bitch.

Even as a kid, I hadn't liked sharing my toys.

We pulled up next to the car and turned off the bikes. The sound of Def Leppard's "Pour Some Sugar On Me" blew out of the hatchback's windows and I exchanged another quick glance with Picnic, who rolled his eyes. I jerked my chin, a silent *fuck you* at the older man. Pic wasn't happy unless he was busting someone's balls, and I wasn't in the mood. Although, I had to admit, it was kind of funny. If I didn't know for a fact Jensen was clueless about our visit, I'd call it a setup. I almost expected a second chick to jump out and start spraying her with a hose, straight out of a goddamn video or something. Best of the '80s, *Trailer Edition Live.*

But the genuine panic on the girl's face said that if Jeff had left her as some sort of peace offering, he hadn't bothered giving her a heads-up first.

I swung a leg over my bike and strolled toward her, eyes trailing across that sweet little body. Yeah, definitely for me—this one was the stuff of wet dreams. Should I fuck her now or after I ripped Jensen a new asshole? I couldn't decide . . . Maybe both. She might not be tall, but those legs were plenty long enough to wrap around my waist. Babe was seriously fine, and I felt my jeans tighten as I closed in on her. My nose flared, taking in her scent.

Damn.

I stopped next to the table, mesmerized and horny as hell. The temperature outside didn't bother me anymore. Neither did the long ride—not with something like this waiting at the end of it. She took deep breaths, chest rising and falling rapidly, and it almost pushed me over the edge. I counted to ten, willing myself not to just grab her and push her down across the table, despite the fact that my cock was 100 percent certain it was the only reasonable course of action. My brain disagreed, and reluctantly I told my cock to shut up.

I wanted to fuck her, not give her a heart attack.

But I needed a little taste.

Just one.

Holding her gaze, I reached out with a finger and traced her collarbone from her shoulder inward, then slid it down between her breasts, grazing her cleavage. I couldn't help myself. She quivered like a deer hit by headlights as I raised the finger to my mouth, tasting her.

Sun and sweat and sweet, ripe woman.

I held back a shudder, and realized I could probably pound nails with my dick. I couldn't remember the last time I'd been this turned on. I'd lost my virginity freshman year in high school to a senior with a taste for younger men. Had I wanted to screw her as bad as this? I wasn't entirely sure, that's how hot Jensen's girl was.

How did such an asshole loser attract a woman like this?

She swallowed nervously and her nipples hardened under their pretty little triangles of fabric. My cock informed me urgently that we really, really needed to be inside her tight little cunt sooner rather than later.

Fuckin' amazing.

Then I saw the bruise. It was old and clearly fading, but someone had backhanded her across the cheek. My breath hissed, and for a second I felt fierce red rage sweep through me, strong enough to override my lust. What could a little thing like her do to possibly justify a man smacking her around? Did Jensen hit her? I clenched my jaw, considering different ways to kill the man. But it was faded, and she hadn't been here last time. Might not be

Jensen. Anyone could've marked her . . . Regardless, whoever was behind the bruise should pay.

Fuckin' crime against nature, smacking around a face like that.

I considered taking her back to Coeur d'Alene for a while—even if he hadn't hit her, Jensen sure as shit wouldn't be able to keep a piece of ass like this satisfied. I'd bet my last dollar on it. Nothing like weed to make a man's dick limp.

I shifted forward into her space, enjoying the way she backed away ever so slightly. Yeah, that was nice. This one wouldn't just roll over for me, and I liked that.

Nothing like a chase to make the kill more satisfying.

"Hey, sweet butt," I said, keeping my voice low and soft. Might as well find out whether she knew jack about bikers. She sure looked like a club whore. I didn't much like the idea of her having been passed around, but if she already knew the rules, it would make life easier. She scrambled backward off the table, and I decided she was probably clueless. I wasn't sure how I felt about that . . . Not an actual club whore, then, which was okay by me. I'd never been a huge fan of used pussy and I already knew I wanted to taste hers. On the other hand, I'd probably have to ease her into things if she didn't know the score.

Fuckin' shame, because I was ready to go.

The girl stood awkwardly, putting the table between us and biting her lip. Small white teeth, ripe red flesh . . . I wanted to suck that lip in, then fuck her mouth with my tongue. No, just fuck her mouth, period. Shit, at this rate I'd blow the fly right off my jeans.

Business first.

I needed to cool off or I'd break her in half when I screwed her. Maybe I should jack off ahead of time? Take off the edge . . . not a bad idea. Her tongue darted, wetting those bright, juicy lips, and I held back a groan.

"Your man here?" I asked, forcing myself to focus. "We need to talk."

A look of confusion crossed her face. The music shut down abruptly. Her eyes darted back behind me, widening as she saw Pic pulling her keys out of the ignition. Then I heard the crunch of gravel as my brothers started toward us, and the confusion on her face shifted back toward panic.

"You mean Jeff? He's in town," she said, paling. She stepped back, putting more space between us, looking toward my fellow Reapers again. "Why don't you wait out here while I call him?"

I studied her, wondering if she was telling the truth. Jensen was just pussy enough to hide behind a woman. Then her eyes drifted down across my cut, like she couldn't help herself. Her gaze felt like fingers against my skin as she checked out my patches, and any lingering doubt I'd had about whether she knew bikers disappeared. She had no clue what it meant when a man put on a cut. I'd definitely have to educate her about my world.

"Sure thing, babe," I said, swinging a leg over the bench to straddle it. She backed away slowly but steadily as Pic and Max joined me.

"How about a drink, girl?" Picnic asked. She nodded and turned toward the trailer, ass twitching as she walked away. Nice view. Max gave a dirty laugh, clearly enjoying the show, and I had to restrain myself from hitting the man.

Asshole should leave my girl alone.

My girl? What the fuck? I didn't have girls. I fucked them and moved on, because life was too damned short to deal with their bullshit. Sure, I was considering leaving with her on the back of my bike, but it wasn't like I'd be keeping her. I just wanted enough time to fuck her out of my system. Where had that thought come from?

"Where do you think Jensen found a bitch like that?" Max asked, and while I'd considered the same question earlier, I didn't like hearing Max call her a bitch. In fact, I didn't want Max calling her anything. I'd never been Max's biggest fan.

"Small town girls," Picnic said. "Not exactly a lot of options. Still, she's too pretty to be scraping bottom. You think he's in there pissing his pants while he hides under the bed?"

I glanced over to the trailer and caught a hint of movement at the window. She peeked through the curtains at me, cell against her ear, looking small and vulnerable. That vulnerability called to me and I licked my lips.

"No, she's making a phone call," I said. "He's not here. I wonder if he'll make a run for it?"

"You think he'd leave her to us?" Max asked, sounding a little too eager. "Hot piece like that should be on her back. Lookin' forward to that."

"Shut it down," Pic said sharply. "She's with Horse now."

"I want her when you're done," Max said, looking at me.

"Shut the fuck up," I snapped, and Max laughed.

"Cockblocker."

"Seriously, Max, shut the fuck up," Picnic replied, his voice like ice.

Silence fell over the table. Then the door to the trailer opened and the woman came out. She held a tall, purple plastic cup in one hand, a smaller cup with a spoon in it in the other, and two more purple cups held against her chest with her arm. She'd changed into a faded T-shirt that had to be at least an extra-large and a pair of those half pants chicks like, the ones that go below the knee. Fuckin' shame, because those curves shouldn't be covered. On the other hand, anything that kept Max's eyes off her was probably a good thing.

"You call your man?" I asked. For reasons I didn't care to examine, figuring out her relationship with Jeff-hole had turned into a high priority.

"My man?" she asked, looking confused.

"Jensen."

She opened her mouth, then closed it, thoughts passing behind her eyes too fast for me to read.

"Girlie, answer the fuckin' question," Picnic commanded, voice like a whip. She jumped, splashing whatever was in the cup across her breast. Her nipple beaded up from the cold and I forgot to breathe. I shifted on the bench, rethinking my decision to wait.

"Jeff's coming," she said. I could just lean forward and catch that nipple in my mouth . . . *Back off.* She was terrified, scaring her more wouldn't move things any faster. I knew how it would end, with her spread under me, screaming when she came. But how long it took to get her there? Lotta ways that could play out. "He said he'd be here in twenty minutes. I've got tea for you."

She stood in front of me, taunting me as she licked her lips nervously. I reached out and took one of the cups. She used the newly free hand to take the smaller cup and glanced toward the table. I smiled. She'd have to lean right across me to set it down. I decided to help her out, reaching over and wrapping my fingers around one of the two cups still clutched against her chest. My fingers grazed her nipple once, twice, and then I took the last cup—the small one, which was full of sugar—and set it on the table.

Our eyes stayed locked as I grasped her hand and pulled her into me, up against my thigh so her stomach almost touched my face. I could smell her, and it took everything I had not to nuzzle her belly. But I needed to know her relationship with Jensen, figure out who had marked her. So instead of pulling her against my mouth, I took her chin and turned it, exposing the bruise fully. I waited for her to say something, but she kept her mouth shut.

Interesting. Was she covering for Jeff?

I dropped my hand back down to her waist, rubbing it up and down the curve of her hip. Those curves were fuckin' perfect, but the way she trembled went straight to my gut. I thought about Jensen, thought about that little fuck touching her soft skin, sucking on those lips . . .

Smacking that pretty face.

Nope, this shit wouldn't stand. Not today.

"Jensen do that to you?"

Her eyes widened and her face flushed.

"No, he'd never do that. Jeff's my brother," she said, jerking free. She turned and ran into the trailer, slamming the door behind her.

"Well, that was interesting," Picnic said. Max chuckled.

I glared at them, then something caught my eye. At the end of the table was a tray with a kitchen towel over it. Two long round lumps lay under it. I leaned over and picked up the towel to find two loaves of unbaked bread rising.

Fuck.

Not only was my girl hot as hell, she could cook, too.

Jensen showed up not long afterward, full of excuses and bullshit.

"Hey, guys, great to see you!" he called as he slammed his car door shut. "I'll bet you're here because of that botched transfer. No worries, Horse, I got it fixed. You can check it on my laptop. I just ran the numbers wrong the first time. No problem."

I stood, crossing my arms as I stared him down.

"Why didn't you answer your phone?"

"I lost it," Jeff replied, rubbing his hands against his pants nervously as he glanced between the three Reapers. "But I found it again. See?"

He pulled it out of his pocket and showed us. I looked to Picnic, who sighed.

"We're gonna lay this out for you, okay?" the club president said. "You fucked up big-time. I don't know if you stole the money and paid it back or if you're just stupid. Either way, it can't happen again. I'm about ready to pull the plug on this little operation, which means pulling the plug on you, stoner boy."

I grunted, seconding his words. Jeff's eyes jerked between us, then settled as he smiled at me again, like we were friends. Fucker had a serious case of reality disconnect.

"No problem," he said. "Let's go inside, I'll show you the figures. Pull 'em up for you, see for yourself. Marie will make dinner, she's a fuckin' great cook. You'll love it."

So her name was Marie. I liked that—it fit her. Sort of old-fashioned but sexy at the same time. I almost smiled, but caught myself. I had a part to play in this little show, and it didn't include looking friendly.

"Let's take a look," I said to Picnic. "Figure it out tonight, save us having to drive back down here to kill him if he's lying."

"Works for me," Pic replied. "I'm hungry. Hey, Jensen—shooting assholes gives me heartburn. Don't fuck this up, 'kay?"

Jeff's face faltered, but he laughed nervously and chattered as he led us into the trailer. Me and Picnic exchanged a knowing look behind his back. I hoped to hell I wouldn't have to kick the shit out of our helpful little hacker. Beating down her brother probably wouldn't be the smoothest way to get into Marie's pants.

The trailer smelled like heaven.

Marinara bubbled on the stove, and while the little window air-conditioning units kept the place cool, the oven sent out homey warmth. Marie stood in the open kitchen, frowning at us as we walked in.

"Sis, my associates are going to stay for dinner," Jeff told her. "You better go get your bread—I think it's done rising. You guys are gonna love this, Marie's bread is amazing. She'll fix you a fuckin' great dinner."

Marie gave her brother a tight, fixed little smile, eyes shooting daggers at him. I had to bite back a laugh—she obviously wanted us gone in a big way. For a minute I thought she might refuse, but then she broke her gaze, murmuring something as she brushed past us to go outside. I couldn't decide if that disappointed me or not. The food smelled great and I hadn't even realized how hungry I'd gotten.

But she should really tell her brother to fuck off—maybe tip that pot of spaghetti sauce over his head or something.

Jeff flicked on his giant-ass TV to mixed martial arts, another layer of bullshit in my opinion. Apparently he could afford a TV the size of a car but he couldn't afford to upgrade to a place fit for his sister to live in.

I shook my head and took a seat in front of the kitchen bar, which separated the cooking area from the living room in the tiny trailer. Leaning back against the wall, I crossed my arms to watch Marie come back inside with the tray of bread, quiet as a mouse. Had the guy who'd hit her broken her spirit? I liked a woman to follow my lead, but a girl without at least a little fight wouldn't be much fun in the sack.

"Grab us some beers, sweet butt," Max called from the couch. I watched as she stilled, biting her lip. I could almost read her thoughts—she wanted to take one of those beer bottles and break it over Max's head. I kinda wanted to see that myself. Instead, she set down the tray on the counter and turned to the fridge, pulling out four drinks and handing them around.

I sighed. Too bad, would've been fun to watch her take Max down. Not that he'd let her go too far with it, but hell . . . bastard could use a bottle over the head.

Marie ignored me as I opened my beer, turning back to put the bread in the oven and then grabbing some shit for a salad. Big fuckin' surprise, watching her cook turned me on. Her clothes looked like hell, but I knew what was underneath and every movement was graceful and feminine. Then she grabbed another beer, popped the top like a pro, and took a deep swig, mouth wrapped tight around the length of the bottle's neck.

I seriously considered vaulting the counter.

Instead, I sat, nursing my drink and counting all the different ways I'd do her before this ended. Over the bar, for sure, from behind. Maybe against the wall. Definitely in the shower and maybe even on my bike. Bed? Why the hell not, some of those missionaries were pretty damn smart. I'd fuck her face, too, and maybe even her ass.

My dick added its vote in favor of that plan and I shifted restlessly.

Goddamn jeans weren't helping the situation.

When Marie pulled the bread out of the oven, the smell almost killed me. Five minutes later she had salad, pasta, and the works laid out on the counter, along with plates.

"Dinner," she said shortly, stepping back as the guys stood and grabbed the food.

The meal blew me away, tasting even better than it smelled. The bread was savory and rich, with a hint of garlic and herbs and something else I couldn't identify. The sauce was chunky and tangy and full of fresh tomatoes with big spicy meatballs. Even the salad was fantastic, and totally different. It had the usual greens, but it also had nuts and fruit and some kind of fancy cheese.

"This is amazing," Picnic told Marie as he filled his plate a second time, voice full of genuine admiration. "You can really cook. My old lady used to cook like this."

That caught my attention. Pic didn't talk about Heather much, and never to strangers. She'd been dead for years, but it could've been yesterday so far as Pic was concerned. He'd given Marie a serious compliment.

She flushed prettily, and murmured, "Thanks."

I held back a frown. I didn't like her blushing and murmuring at another guy.

Fuckin' Picnic.

The food was gone all too soon, though I'd definitely gotten my fill. Hell, I should bring her back to Coeur d'Alene just to cook—woman had a gift. Picnic caught my eye and jerked his head toward Marie. I sighed.

Time to check out Jeff's story and then scare the crap out of him.

I was ready to finish this particular game. I'd joined the club for the freedom and the fun, and now I found myself managing some hacker asshat like a goddamn human resources officer. Bullshit all around. Might as well get a job down at city hall, buy a suit, and trade my bike for a minivan.

"You might want to go for a drive," I told Marie, wishing it didn't need to happen. I'd wait for her to get back, but still . . . lotta ways for things to go wrong under the circumstances. "We've got business."

"Do you mind, sis?" Jeff asked. She shook her head, looking almost wistful. Then she pulled herself together and smiled at us—that same bright, fake smile she'd given earlier—as she went to the door and grabbed her purse.

"Well, nice to meet all of you, um . . ."

Picnic stood and offered a wolfish grin. I didn't care for that one bit—I'd have words with him later.

"I'm Picnic, and these are my brothers, Horse and Max."

Marie looked at me, her expression puzzled. I raised a brow, waiting to see what she'd do next. Ask about my name, maybe? Nope, she was chickening out.

"Nice to meet you, Mr. Picnic," she said.

"Just Picnic. Thanks again for the food."

There was that admiring tone in his president's voice again. Time to shut it down.

"I'll walk you out to your car," I said, voice firm. Pic gave me a knowing look and I realized the man had been fucking with me.

Again.

Asshole.

"Take your time, we can wait," Pic said, pulling Marie's car keys from his pocket and tossing them to her. She stepped out of the trailer, me right behind her. The door slammed shut, the warm evening air surrounded us, and I felt myself relax. Dealing with Jensen was a pain in the ass, but it would be worth it because I planned on having a hell of a good time with his sister before I was finished.

I snagged her hand, pulling her toward the table, turning and tucking my hands under her arms to pop her onto the end. She stared up at me, blinking rapidly as I slid my hands down her sides, wedging them between her legs and pushing her knees gently apart. Then I leaned into her, inhaling her scent once more.

Marie smelled even better now than before, with a hint of fresh bread added into the mix. I gave serious thought to biting her shoulder, just to see if she tasted half as good as that scent of hers suggested.

"I don't think this is a good idea," she said, her voice quavering. She pulled away from me, glancing toward the trailer. "I mean, everyone is waiting for you, right? I can just go, let's forget this, okay?"

I leaned back, studying her, wishing I felt half as unaffected as she seemed to be. If she didn't want me touching her, why would she let me hold her like this? This tension between us was incredible. It couldn't only be on my side. Could it?

The fading evening light caught on her bruise.

Fuck.

Maybe her spirit really was totally broken. I decided to poke at her and test whether she'd fight back, even a little.

"That how you gonna play it, sweet butt?" I asked, deliberately taunting her. Her eyes narrowed and flashed. Sexy as hell.

"I'm not your sweet butt," she snapped. "Fuck off."

Now that was more like it—my girl hadn't checked out entirely after all. I laughed, loving the spark in her and wanting to see more of it. That wasn't all I wanted, though. I grabbed her waist and pulled her into my body. The hot, welcoming softness of her pussy hit my cock and it felt better than I'd imagined, which was saying something. I closed my eyes for a second, swiveling my hips and dragging my length up and down across her clit through the fabric of our pants, all but tasting the moment I'd sink into her sweet opening.

It was official.

Marie was the hottest piece of ass I'd ever met.

She gasped as I slid my dick against her again, more forcefully this time. I leaned down into her and blew softly on her ear, thinking about kissing her. Then I thought about that spark of anger in her eyes—I wanted to see it again. Marie soft and willing beneath me was great, but Marie telling me to fuck off, all cute and pissy?

Now that *really* turned me on.

"Nice ass. Sweet. Butt," I whispered softly.

She bit me.

Hard.

I jumped back, ripping my ear out of her mouth, wondering if she'd taken a chunk with her. Holy shit—she *bit* me. A trickle of warm fluid ran down my neck. Blood. I couldn't help it, I burst out laughing because she was tiny and angry and hissing at me like a wet cat on top of the table. I wanted to fuck her more now than I had five minutes ago. Damn, though . . . my ear hurt. That wasn't a love bite.

Who was this woman?

Marie scowled, her message coming through loud and clear.

"I get it, hands off," I said, shaking my head, holding up my arms in pointed surrender. My dick might not be amused by this turn of events, but for once I didn't give a flying fuck what my dick wanted. I was having way too much fun. "Play it the way you like. And you're right, we've got business. Go drive for an hour, that should be enough time."

Marie slid off the table, darting around me as she ran to her little piece-of-shit car. I followed, bemused, wondering if she had some magic power that turned grown men into pussies. Marie opened her car door but turned back to look at me, teeth worrying at her lip. I waited for whatever the hell would come out of her mouth. After that bite, I was on uncharted ground. At least it wasn't boring.

"Horse isn't your real name, is it?"

I smiled. Now *that* was better . . . Playtime wasn't over yet, after all.

"Road name," I replied. "That's the way things work in my world. Citizens have names. We have road names."

"What does that mean?"

"People give them to you when you start riding. They can mean all kinds of things. Picnic got his name because he went all out planning some pansy-assed picnic for a bitch who had him twisted up in knots. She ate his food and drank his booze, then called her fuckwad boyfriend to come and pick her up while he took a leak."

She frowned.

"That seems . . . unpleasant. Why would he want to remember that?"

"Because when the fuckwad showed up, Picnic shoved his head through a picnic table."

Her breath caught and I saw indecision written all over her face.

"And Max?"

"When he gets drunk, sometimes his eyes go all wide and he looks fuckin' crazy, like Mad Max."

"I see," she said, glancing toward the trailer. I waited, but she kept her mouth closed. Smart girl. I'd be damned if I'd let her off the hook that easy, though.

"So aren't you gonna ask?" Silence fell between us, then she opened her mouth.

"So why are you called Horse?"

"'Cause I'm hung like one," I replied, unable to control my smirk. She blushed hard and ducked in the car. I had to jump back and away as she jammed it into gear and peeled out of the driveway.

Now *that* was fun.

And weird.

I still wanted to nail her, probably more now than before. But that little exchange—bite and all—that'd been better than the average blow job.

Go figure.

***

"The money's all there," I said, clicking through the list of accounts. I glanced over at Jeff, who sat by the kitchen bar smoking a little glass pipe. He'd gone from jittery to stoned in the time I'd been outside with Marie. Hadn't seen that coming. Pic must've really wanted the asshole to shut up, because normally he'd never tolerate someone getting faded before business was finished.

"Of course it's all there," Jeff said lazily. "I already told you. It was just a little mistake and I fixed it. I don't know why you got so worked up about it."

"I got worked up because I thought you were stealing," I replied. "And you know what happens to people who steal from the club. We need to go over the rules again?"

Jeff took a long hit, then started coughing, smoke shooting out of his nose in little puffs. He grabbed his beer and sucked it down before answering.

"You don't have to keep threatening me. I knew what I was getting into. We've been working together for nearly two years and I've never screwed you, have I? Trust needs to go both ways."

Max snorted and for once I didn't consider telling him to shut up.

"Tell me about your sister."

Jeff's face sobered and he set down his pipe.

"Marie's been through a lot," he replied. "She doesn't need any more trouble, Horse."

"Who hit her?"

"Her husband," Jeff said. "Always hated him. She left his ass, thank God. She deserves a little happiness. No offense, but I'd really appreciate it if you'd leave her alone."

"Now you're telling me what to do?"

Jeff straightened, and for the first time in a year he looked almost like a man instead of a weasel.

"She's a good girl, Horse," he said firmly. "She's been through hell, she's finally free, and she doesn't need anyone new in her life. She needs to get a divorce and go to school and then meet some nice guy with a steady job who'll treat her like a queen. Let it go."

"Damn, that almost sounded like something a decent human being would say," Max muttered. "I think we may have a body snatchers situation going on here."

"Think what you like," Jeff said, shrugging. "But it's the truth. She's rid of Gary and pretty soon she's gonna realize she's free to do anything she wants. I won't have her wasting that freedom on some biker who'll treat her like shit. And don't bother waiting for her to come back. I already texted her and told her to stay away."

I shrugged, not entirely surprised. When a chick bit my ear and told me to fuck off, it wasn't usually a sign I'd be getting laid that night. My cock might be pissed about it, but I'd started to realize just how much more I wanted from Marie. Hot pussy crawled out of the woodwork at the club, nothing special about it . . .

A sweet girl like her was a hell of a lot harder to find.

Jeff sat waiting, apparently expecting some sort of violent outburst, so I gave him a nice big smile, just to fuck with his head.

"Tell her I said good-bye," I told him. "I'll be back before long to check up on things. I've got what I need, should be able to monitor the rest from home."

I looked to my brothers to make sure he hadn't missed something. Max cracked his knuckles and Picnic nodded, satisfied.

"I don't want to breathe in any more of Jeff-hole's secondhand smoke," I said. "You ready, Pic?"

"Sure," Picnic replied, and Max pulled himself up off the couch, stretching. Thankfully, Jeff kept his stupid mouth shut as we went outside.

Night had fallen, and while the air was still warm, it didn't hold the punishing heat we'd experienced earlier. Riding home across the desert wouldn't be half bad.

I kicked my bike to life, following my club president down the long driveway through the apple trees.

Hadn't been such a shitty trip after all.

Hopefully, Marie wouldn't tear up my other ear too bad during our next fight.

MARIE'S BREAD RECIPE

Ingredients

4 ½ teaspoons (or two packets) of rapid rise yeast
2 ½ cups warm water
1 tablespoon salt
1 tablespoon olive oil
7 cups all-purpose flour
2 handfuls mixed grated cheese (your choice—I often just grab an Italian mix)
1/4 cup (approximately) grated parmesan
2 large spoonfuls chopped garlic (slightly less if using fresh garlic, although I often use the prepared chopped garlic in a bottle for convenience—if it's a squeeze bottle, I do two very large gloops)
Italian herb mix
1 egg white mixed with 1 tablespoon cold water
Corn meal

Preparation

Note: I use a Kitchenaid mixer with a dough hook to make bread. If you make the bread by hand, follow basic bread dough preparation instructions out of any cookbook.

Put warm water and yeast in mixing bowl and allow to proof (3-4 minutes). Follow with flour and salt, then add in oil, two handfuls of cheese, garlic, and a generous shake of Italian herb mix. (I've never measured this, but don't be afraid to pour it on—the recipe makes two loaves of bread, which means you want to put in plenty.) Allow dough hook to mix until the bread is fully kneaded. (About four minutes on my machine.)

Place bread in a greased bowl and allow to double in size. Punch down, then divide into two parts. Using a rolling pin, spread each dough ball out into a rectangle, then roll up along the long side to create a skinny loaf. Place on a baking pan that's been lined with foil, greased, and sprinkled with cornmeal. (Be sure the seam is on the bottom.) Allow to rise until double in size.

Before baking bread, make four thin slices diagonally across the top to give it some texture, then sprinkle with parmesan. Bake at 450 for 20 minutes, then remove from oven. Brush with egg white mixed with cold water to create a glaze. Cook for an additional five minutes then allow to cool before slicing.

AUTHOR'S NOTE: *The top request I get from readers is for a short story about Horse and Marie, telling what happened to them after* Reaper's Property. *"Skunked" is that story. If you haven't read* Reaper's Property, *you can still read "Skunked"—it doesn't have any plot spoilers, aside from the fact that* Reaper's Property *ended with them together as a couple, which shouldn't come as a huge surprise for most romance readers.*

"Skunked" takes place several years after the end of Reaper's Property. *I got the idea late one night after something rather unpleasant happened with our dog . . .*

SKUNKED

HORSE

Christ, I couldn't remember the last time I'd been this tired.

We'd been on a five-day run to Boise and had spent the night before camped out. I was tired, grumpy, and more than a little horny—something that hadn't gone unnoticed by the bitch who'd kept grabbing for my cock at the last clubhouse we'd visited. I'd managed to fight her off, but this celibacy shit was getting old.

I wanted my old lady, and I wanted her now.

Turning down our driveway, I saw Marie's car in front of the house. She hadn't answered her phone all day—this wasn't like her. I'd assumed if something was really wrong, someone would've gotten hold of me. Still, it was a relief to find her at home. I wanted a cold beer, a hot shower, and a blow job.

Could only accomplish two of the three on my own.

Parking my bike, I decided to leave my saddlebags for now and head toward the house. The door wasn't locked. I stepped into the living room, looking around for her. The lights were on and so was the TV, but no sign of my girl.

"Marie?"

Nothing.

I passed through the living room and started down the hallway toward the kitchen.

"Babe, you in here?"

"In the back," she replied, her voice faint. Entering the kitchen, I knew something was wrong as soon as I saw her face. Her eyes were red and puffy, and she seemed out of it—almost dazed.

"What the fuck's going on?" I asked. She jumped, looking toward me with something like fear in her expression. Jesus, had someone hurt her? A burst of adrenaline rushed through me—nobody touched my woman. I'd fucking kill them. She didn't say anything, though. "Marie?"

She shook herself, almost as if she needed to wake up.

"Sorry, I was sort of lost in my thoughts."

"What's going on?"

She stared at me for several seconds, her mouth tight. "We need to talk."

Great—words every man loves to hear. So much for my "welcome home" blow job.

"About what?" I asked warily.

"Sit down," she murmured, glancing away from me. "You want a beer?"

Up to that point, a beer had been damned high on my list of priorities. Now? Not so much. I pulled out a chair at the big wooden block that served as our kitchen table and sat down with a thump, leaning back. Then I crossed my arms over my chest.

"So let's talk," I told her, forcing myself to stay patient. Marie swallowed, then reached for the cup of tea sitting on the block in front of her, taking a nervous sip.

"Okay, so here goes," she said quietly, refusing to look at me. "We've got some big changes ahead of us. You need to remember that it just happened, babe. It's not like I did it on purpose. Please remember that."

She shot me another quick look, her face full of dread. Put that together with the puffy eyes and I realized we were in the shit. Deep shit. Had she cheated on me? Rage roared through my soul, drowning out my ability to think.

Whoever the fuck the guy was, I wouldn't just kill him. I'd kill him slow. Wasn't sure what I'd do to Marie. Jesus. Never saw it coming, not even for a minute. I'd thought my wife was happy.

"Tell me," I ordered her, my voice cold. I forced the feelings down, burying them deep under a layer of ice. *Hold it together, don't do anything stupid 'til you hear her out.*

"Okay, so while you were gone I—"

A piercing howl tore through the kitchen from behind the house, followed by a series of agonized, terrifying yelps.

Marie's eyes widened and she jumped to her feet. "That was Ariel!"

Another howl tore through the air. Sure as shit, she was right—that was definitely our dog. Good God, of all the fucking times for the mutt to go apeshit. Marie was halfway to the door when I caught her, instinctively jerking her behind my body as I pulled out my gun.

"Stay inside," I told her. "Could be anything."

Full of dark purpose, I reached for the door handle—irony, anyone? Here I was, ready to do anything to protect this woman, even though she'd probably cheated on me. *Fuck it.* Opening the door, I looked outside cautiously.

The smell hit me first.

Jesus.

Christ.

Skunk. *Fucking dog had found a skunk.* The harsh reality sank in as Marie moaned behind me.

"That is the worst smell on earth," she said. There was a rustling in the bushes, and then Ariel burst out into the open, racing toward us.

"Down!" I shouted at him, because the dog was about two seconds from jumping me and then I'd reek, too. Ariel fell back cowering, whining up at us even as waves of stench radiated off of his body.

The stink was strong. *Seriously* strong. My eyes started burning and I felt the tiny hairs inside my nose standing straight up. I opened my mouth, hoping that bypassing my nose might do some good. This only made things worse because now I could taste it.

"I think I'm gonna puke," Marie whispered behind me. "Shit, what should we do? Have you ever had to clean skunk off him before?"

I shook my head, frustration mixing with the anger that still filled me. "No, I remember my mom cleaning off a dog when I was a kid, but I've been lucky out here. I've smelled skunks but never had one get too close to the house. Fuck, I got no idea what we should do. Hose him off?"

"I don't think that's a good idea. Let me look it up, see what I can find."

"We could just shoot him," I grunted, glancing down at my gun. "Of course, we'd still have to deal with a skunked dog corpse."

"Please tell me you aren't serious."

I glanced back to find her holding a hand over her mouth. There was a distinctly green tinge to her skin, and as I watched, she gagged.

"Just go look it up," I said, the words short. "I'll stay out here, keep him calm."

She stepped back into the house, and I blinked, eyes still watering. It wasn't just a smell. No. This was a tangible, evil presence wafting around my body like something out of a horror movie.

After what felt like hours, Marie stuck her head out the door again.

"I found a recipe."

"Tomato juice?" I asked. "Or is that just an urban legend?"

"They say tomato juice does nothing. But we can blot him with paper towels, and then wash him with a mixture of hydrogen peroxide, baking soda, and detergent—there's lots of sources saying that it works."

"Do we have the stuff?" I said, frowning at the dog. How long would it take to wear off? Probably weeks . . . *Fuck*.

"Yeah, we have everything except rubber gloves," she said. "I could go to town and get them, but apparently there's about a ten minute window. At that point, the smell will set in and then we'll be screwed. We're supposed to start by blotting off the oils."

I closed my eyes, a condemned man.

"Give me the paper towels."

"Wait."

"What?"

"Take off your club colors first," she said softly. "Otherwise you'll get skunk on them."

Shit—that'd go over just great at the clubhouse. I turned toward her, tucking the gun back into my pants. Then I pulled off my leather vest with my Reapers MC patches on it. Folding it carefully, I started to hand it to her, then hesitated. Marie waited, frowning at me, and I thought about what she'd said earlier. Had she cheated on me?

The dog had distracted me for a minute, but now the anger came flooding back.

"What were you going to tell me?" I asked her bluntly.

"Let's take care of the dog first," she replied, eyes dropping. "We've only got a few minutes, Horse. The stink is already working its way down into his fur. We need more time for this discussion, okay?"

No, it wasn't okay. Ariel whined, and the unholy smell grew stronger as he crept forward to lean heavily against my leg. Marie gagged again, eyes blinking rapidly from the fumes.

Fumes or guilt?

"Tell me the fucking truth. Did you—"

Marie's face twisted and then she turned away and started retching. I reached for her hair, planning to hold it back or something, but then I remembered I was pissed at her so I stood back. Ariel whined again, flopping to his back and showing his stomach.

Frustration burned through me, and suddenly I couldn't keep still.

"Goddammit!" I shouted, kicking the side of the concrete steps. The dog cringed harder as a wave of intense pain radiated up my leg. Fucking hell, had I just broken my toe? Sure as shit felt like it. Marie heaved again, then managed to stand up, wiping off her mouth with the bottom of her shirt.

"I'm sorry," she whispered, but I'd had enough.

"Get me the fucking paper towels," I yelled. "And make up the cleaning shit!"

She ran into the house, returning less than a minute later with a roll of paper towels. I shoved my cut at her, snatching the towels and plastic garbage bag out of her hands in an awkward shuffle. Marie disappeared back inside, still gagging.

Leaning down, I started blotting the dog. You'd think my sense of smell would have deadened by now. No such luck. The towels soaked up the oily spray, which seemed to have hit the dog square in the face, transferring it to my fingers in the process. My eyes watered and I wondered how well the stupid mixture Marie was fixing would actually work.

This fucking sucked.

"Here's the cleaner," Marie said, stepping back outside. She carried a large glass measuring bowl that had a handle and spout. A milky, watery mixture sloshed inside, along with two kitchen sponges.

"Bring it here," I snapped, wondering if I'd ever get the taste of skunk out of my mouth. Marie set it on the ground next to me, kneeling as she grabbed a sponge and raised it to Ariel's sad face.

"The article said to be careful of his eyes," she told me, starting on his nose. I picked up the other sponge and started working on his ear. This wasn't exactly made easier by him slithering around on his back, as if our attempts to clean him were the cruelest torture in history.

"I'm being careful," I replied through gritted teeth, squeezing the sponge. The mix squirted out of it, straight toward his eye. Marie glared at me, reaching for a paper towel to dab around the area. The dog blinked, but thankfully he seemed to have closed his eyes in time. Marie gagged again.

"What the fuck is wrong with you?" I demanded. "It's a fucking skunk, deal with it."

"It's making me feel sick," she said, narrowing her eyes at me. Great, now *she* was getting pissy? I was the victim here. "It smells bad, okay? I can't help it."

"You don't see me puking," I snarled. Ariel moaned.

"You're scaring the dog!"

Oh, fuck her.

"I come home to find you cheated on me, and now you're giving me a lecture?"

Marie's mouth dropped.

"Excuse me?" she asked, her voice a dangerously low whisper.

"You heard what I said."

"You fucking asshole," she sneered, shaking her head slowly. "I didn't cheat on you, Horse. Although maybe I *should,* since you obviously don't trust me for shit. Of course, attracting another guy might be a little difficult, seeing as I'm currently *carrying your child.*"

The bottom dropped out of my stomach. Marie nodded slowly, a nasty smile twisting her mouth. "Yeah, you heard me right. I'm the pregnant one and you're the asshole. So, far as I know, neither of us is a cheater, although I find it a little unnerving that that's the first place your mind went. It's been a weird day, Horse. I took the test about half an hour before you got home—after puking my guts out for the last ten hours. It's a bit of a mind fuck, and I was trying to figure out the best way to tell you, since we'd agreed that we would wait a couple more years. Surprise, Horse. You're gonna be a daddy."

Then she flipped me off and I had to concede the point.

I was a total asshole.

"You're seriously pregnant?" I asked slowly, sitting back on my heels. The anger had disappeared, but the adrenaline still swirled around me, making it impossible to think.

"Yes," Marie said, rinsing out her sponge as she started working down Ariel's side carefully. "Can you help me get him up? We have to get his back, and I'm worried he'll grind the oils in if he keeps doing this."

I stared at her blankly. "We need to talk."

Marie rolled her eyes.

"No shit. I think I mentioned something about that, remember?"

I winced, thinking about what I'd said to her.

"I'm sorry."

"And I'm cleaning a dog covered in skunk oils that have another two or three minutes before they set in," she replied pointedly. "You know, *your* dog? Stop just sitting there and help clean Ariel."

"He's your dog, too," I protested, then shut my eyes, wondering what the hell was wrong with me. I couldn't *think*. There was a baby inside Marie. My baby. Holy fuck, there was gonna be a baby coming out of her and it would be my kid.

Mine.

I pictured her holding a little pink infant, nursing it in the living room while I stood over them protectively. The thought of it was enough to cut through the fog, and I had a sudden, magnificent realization.

"Your tits are gonna get huge," I blurted out.

Marie sat back, blinking at me.

"You accuse me of cheating while we're scrubbing skunk off the dog, I tell you you're going to be a father, and all you can think about are my tits?"

I shook my head at her slowly. "Marie, babe . . . you know I think about your tits all the time."

Ariel snorted and the stench rose thick between us. Marie shook her head slowly, and for long seconds I thought I was screwed. Then I caught the first hint of a smile. A real smile.

"You're hopeless," she said quietly.

"I know what I like," I countered, grinning back at her. "You're gorgeous, you know—it fucks with my head, and I'm kind of a moron to begin with. How far along are you?"

"I think about ten weeks, although I'm not totally sure. I had my last two periods, but they were really light. Spotting, more than anything. That threw me off."

"This is amazing," I said, feeling my stupid smile getting bigger. My baby. I wondered if the kid would be a boy or girl. Fuck, did it matter? "Christ, I love you."

Leaning forward over the dog, I tried to kiss her. Panic crossed her face, and then she was turning again, gagging and heaving.

"You have morning sickness," I realized. She ignored me, and Ariel whined, staring at us with big, sad eyes. I needed to get moving. If we didn't get the dog clean, the smell would stick around for weeks—Marie couldn't handle that.

Not with morning sickness.

"Go inside," I told her. "Just strip off your clothes out here and I'll take care of them. Clean up and go to bed—you need rest."

She pushed herself up and rolled her eyes, weak but determined.

"No, I want to help you," she said. "Despite you being a dumbass, we're in this together. If you smell, I smell."

"You're crazy," I said bluntly. "No sane person chooses skunk over bed, so get those clothes off and go inside. My baby hates skunk smell. Don't fuck it up for him."

Marie laughed.

"And how would you know that?" she asked, raising a brow.

"*Everyone* hates skunk smell. Just go . . . be pregnant somewhere. Wherever it smells the least."

Marie rolled her eyes.

"Horse?"

"Yeah?"

"It's not even nine p.m. yet," she pointed out gently. "I'm knocked up, not a hundred years old. And you need help—we're running out of time."

Fuck. I looked down at the dog, whose mouth lolled open in a grin. Then his tongue caught a taste of the skunk-cleanser mix, and suddenly he was twisting his head around, smacking his lips, trying to get rid of it.

"I'm killing you when we're done here," I told him.

Ariel gave me an anxious whine.

Marie laughed, grabbing her sponge as she started scrubbing again. I wanted to push the point with her, but she was right—we were out of time—so I grabbed my own sponge. I lifted it to the dog's side, watching as it bubbled up through his fur, hopefully taking the stink out with it. My mind was still racing, though.

Marie was pregnant.

I'd been a jealous asshole.

Babies were scary.

Marie's tits were gonna get *huge.*

"You're thinking about my boobs again, aren't you?" she asked.

I looked up at her, busted. "No."

She raised a brow, and I shrugged because of course I was thinking about her boobs, and we both knew it.

"It's okay—I'm kind of excited about it, too."

"Then why were you crying?" I asked, suddenly remembering what she'd looked like when I'd come in. "You do want the baby, don't you?"

"Of course I want the baby," she said, her face puzzled. "And I didn't even realize I was crying. Must've been the hormones or something. But I was nervous about telling you—this isn't what we planned."

I shrugged.

"Waiting was your plan, not mine. I just wanted you to be ready before we started trying, that's all."

"So you're ready to be a daddy?" she asked, looking up at me. "Because it's a big deal . . . Everything is going to change for us."

"Life is change," I pointed out. "And I like the idea of you all big and round with my kid in you—it's cute."

Marie frowned. "I'm gonna get fat."

Now it was my turn to roll my eyes.

"Carrying a baby is not the same as getting fat," I pointed out reasonably. "And I think it's sexy."

"You get turned on by pregnant chicks?" she asked, her voice dry. "I know you're a perv, but this is a new one. How long have you had this fetish?"

Dipping my sponge back into the mix, I laughed.

"Don't worry, it's recent—specific to you. I'm fuckin' crazy about you, babe. You know that, right?"

Marie smiled at me, and I swear to God, she started glowing like some pregnant lady cliché, right in front of me. Beautiful. My beautiful, beautiful girl . . .

"I love you," I said, my voice dead serious.

"I love you, too," she whispered back. "I even love your dog. But let's get him clean, sound good?"

Nodding, I agreed, although the smell wasn't even bothering me that much anymore. How could it, after getting news like this?

***

By the time we finished, we reeked. Both of us.

I had a feeling it was worse than we realized, because I'm pretty sure at least half the nerves in my nose had committed suicide. Our clothes were outside in the plastic garbage bag, along with the paper towels and the sponges. I'd wanted to throw away the bowl, too, just on general principles, but Marie wouldn't let me.

Apparently pregnancy can make women stubborn.

"I can't believe I didn't think of closing the windows," Marie mumbled around a mouthful of toothpaste as I stepped out of the shower. She sat on the toilet, still wrapped in a towel from her own shower. Normally we'd clean up together, but tonight she was obviously exhausted, and I wasn't sure I could handle a slippery, naked Marie without fucking her. Hell, I was so tired I'd probably drop her or something. Not that being exhausted had ever slowed me down before, but things had changed.

There were three of us now.

Right on cue, I felt that dumbass grin take over my face again.

"It's not that bad, we can handle it," I said, shrugging. She raised a brow.

"Go into the bedroom, and then tell me that again."

I wrapped the towel around my waist and stepped out into the hallway, heading toward our room. As soon as I opened the door, I realized she was right—we'd fucked up. The windows had been open on all three sides when the skunk hit, and now the place was so thick with stench that you could practically see toxic green tendrils hanging in the air. The windows were still wide open, which I guess made sense at this point—the damage was done.

Fucking great.

Walking over to the dresser, I found a pair of briefs and pulled them on, followed by jeans and a shirt. Then I grabbed one of Marie's pretty panty and bra sets (damn, but I loved those) and a sundress before heading back to the bathroom.

"Here you go," I told her, setting them on the counter. Then I turned away, because the last thing she needed was me shoving my dick in her face. (And now I was thinking about my cock in her mouth . . . Fucking great—I officially had the worst timing on earth.) "I settled Ariel out in the barn for the night. We're gonna go get a hotel room."

"We don't need to do that."

She stood up, and I turned to find her dressed.

"You're knocked up, you puked all day, and the house smells like a skunk died in it. We're getting a hotel room."

Marie walked over to me, then wrapped her arms around my waist and leaned her head against my chest.

"Are we really okay?" she asked, her voice a whisper.

I hugged her back, running one hand up and down her back.

"No, we aren't okay," I said softly. "We're trapped in a skunk house full of toxic fumes. But once we get away from here, I think things will be perfect. And just think about what a great story we'll have to tell the kiddo."

Her hand slipped down to my ass, giving it a squeeze, and I groaned.

"Speaking of, you sure you don't wanna celebrate the baby before we head out?"

Groaning, I caught her butt and pulled her into me, rubbing my dick against her stomach. God, I wanted to be inside her . . . Then it hit me—my kid was inside her, too. Right next to where I planned to shove my cock. I jerked away, because that was a mind fuck I wasn't quite ready for. Shit. I'd have to find a way to wrap my brain around that.

"What's wrong?" she asked, frowning. I shook my head, realizing this wasn't a conversation we needed to have just yet.

"Nothing's wrong," I said quickly, staring down into her face. Her brown eyes were deep and her beautiful, curly brown hair was hanging around her face and across her shoulders. God, but I loved this woman. Right on cue, my dick made its needs known, and I realized that wrapping my head around things might not be so difficult after all . . . I just needed to let the right head do the thinking.

I grinned, leaning over to kiss the tip of Marie's nose. Then I grabbed her hand and pulled her toward the stairs. The sooner we found a room, the sooner we could celebrate. "C'mon. Let's get the hell out of here. I've had enough of being skunked."

MARIE'S EMERGENCY SKUNK SOLUTION

NOTE: *Don't let the dog wait in the house while you mix up the solution. Seriously. Also, some people (Mr. Wylde among them) feel that cleaning up after a skunk goes a little more smoothly if you have a very strong drink available. Straws help, allowing for hands-free access.*

Supplies

Rubber gloves, preferably long ones
Paper towels (or tissues in a pinch)
Plastic garbage bags

Ingredients

1 quart hydrogen peroxide
¼ cup baking soda
1 tablespoon liquid dish soap

Preparation

Mix all ingredients in a bowl. Put on gloves and use paper towels to blot as much skunk oil off the dog as possible, throwing them into the plastic bag as soon as you finish. Do your best not to allow the dog to brush against you or transfer the oils. Using a washcloth or sponge, gently rinse the hydrogen peroxide mixture through the dog's fur two times, mixing up more as needed. (Avoid the dog's eyes, and flush with water if the mix gets into the eyes.) Rinse the dog with water thoroughly. You will notice that he still smells like wet dog and a bit skunky, but it will be a huge improvement (when a skunk first sprays, the smell is so powerful that it burns your eyes and nose). Remove your clothing and dispose of gloves while still outside, if possible.

Allow dog to sleep in garage, enclosed porch, or bathroom (somewhere well ventilated and safe, but not part of the main section of your house). By morning, the dog will be dry and very little skunk scent will be noticeable.

AUTHOR'S NOTE: *This is a prequel short story about the first time Melanie and Painter met. Their book,* Reaper's Fall, *will be published on Nov. 10, 2015. "Sugar and Spice" takes place one year before the beginning of* Reaper's Fall, *against the background of action from Reaper's Stand. I thought you might enjoy reading it.*

SUGAR AND SPICE

MELANIE

I fell for Levi "Painter" Brooks the first time I saw him, although in all fairness I did have a head injury at the time.

It was a weird start to a relationship, too.

You see, I blew up a house.

It wasn't on purpose, and in my defense I'd had a really shitty day. My mom had taken off earlier in the week. Just up and left while I was at work on Monday, and she never came back. Neither me or my dad heard a thing from her, and while she'd always been sort of flaky, she'd never done anything like this before. By Wednesday night, I broke down and asked him if we should report her missing to the police.

He'd thrown his beer bottle at me, shouting about how "the whore" must've gotten herself a new man. She'd left me because I was nothing, just like she was nothing.

Then he'd told me to go buy him more beer. I decided to call Loni instead.

Not long afterward, I blew up her house.

***

London Armstrong was my best friend's aunt. Jessica and I had been tight for years, and as my own mother drifted further and further from reality, they'd become my second family. She'd told me to head on over to her place and let myself in, that she'd see me later that night. I went over there and made myself some macaroni and cheese on her gas stove.

A couple hours later the house exploded.

Gas leak.

Nobody said it was my fault, but I knew it had to be. I'd been the last one to use the stove, so there you have it. Anyway, fate has a weird sense of humor, because that's how I met Painter. The next day, I mean. At the hospital.

He gave me a lift on his motorcycle, and I fell in love. God I was young. Young and stupid.

***

"I sort of thought you meant a car when you said you'd give me a ride home," I whispered, staring at the tall, beautiful, terrifyingly perfect man standing in front of a shiny black Harley with custom gold trim. He'd been introduced to me as Painter, and apparently he was part of the same motorcycle club as Loni's new boyfriend, Reese.

"She did have a head injury," London pointed out, her voice tart. She held my arm protectively, staring between me and Painter with worry written all over her face.

"Sort of thought the car was implied," said Reese, sighing.

"You didn't say and it's not like she's really hurt or anything," Painter replied with a shrug. He glanced at me. "You got a headache?" I did, but he was so pretty and perfect and I didn't want to jinx this. Blond, spiky hair. Strong, straight cheekbones and muscular arms that I just knew would be strong enough to pick up a girl like me and carry me wherever I needed to go.

"No, I don't actually," I said, feeling nervous but excited, too. I shot another look at the bike, imagining what it would feel like to sit behind him, holding him as we flew down the highway. "Although they said no sudden movements."

"So you'll hold on tight," Painter said, eyes playing with mine. He licked his lip and I felt my insides twitch.

Ohmygodhe'ssohotandhe'slookingrightatme!

"Oh, for fuck's sake," Reese said, reaching into his pocket for his phone. "I'll call someone else."

"No, it's okay," I said quickly, hoping Mr. Hot Bod wouldn't change his mind about giving me a ride. "I'll try riding the bike."

I'll try riding you, sexy . . .

Wow. Those kind of pervy thoughts weren't like me at all. Painter winked and I would've fainted on the spot if I wasn't so damned healthy and not the fainting type. Shame, too, because he'd totally catch me with those muscular arms of his. I could sense it. I gave him a little smile, hoping I wasn't coming off as dorky.

"You watch yourself with her," London snapped, crossing her arms and jutting out a hip. I stared at her, shocked—that wasn't like Loni at all. Had she just ruined it for me?

Painter raised a brow.

"Fuckin' priceless, prez," he said, then smiled at me again, a smile so beautiful that it made me dizzy. *You're dizzy because you have a concussion,* my common sense pointed out.

I gave it a mental finger, because fuck common sense.

"You comin' or not?" he asked, swaggering over to his bike and climbing on. Deliberately avoiding London's gaze, I followed him, hopping up behind before he had a chance to change his mind.

"Hold on, babe," he told me, his voice low and smooth. Like whiskey. Not that I drank much whiskey, but I'd had some at our high school graduation party, at the beginning of the summer. Putting my hands up, I touched the sides of his hips hesitantly. He caught them, pulling them tight around his stomach. I could feel his hard abs through the thin fabric of his shirt, and smell the leather of his motorcycle vest thingie. My entire front was leaning against his entire back, and I felt dizzy again. Then he reached down and touched my knee, giving it a quick squeeze.

Oh. My. God.

***

The ride took about ten minutes. Ten glorious minutes that included a short stretch of highway as we left Coeur d'Alene behind, which meant we got to go *fast.* Then he was pulling off and parking in front of an old farmstead that had a well-lived in, well-loved kind of wear around the edges. He turned off the bike, and the sudden absence of noise and vibration left my ears ringing. We sat there for a minute as I collected my thoughts. He touched my knee again. "Gotta let go if you want off the bike, babe," he said softly.

I jerked my hands back instantly, wondering how big of an ass I'd made of myself. Then I was scrambling to get off, looking everywhere but his face because I couldn't bear to see him looking disgusted, or worse yet, sorry for me.

"Come on," he said, touching the small of my back gently, guiding me toward the porch. "I've got the code to get you inside. You can go crash for a while, get some rest."

"Thanks," I said, daring to look up at him. His eyes were everywhere, scanning the yard for what, I had no idea. Five minutes later we were upstairs, looking at what had to be a girl's bedroom.

"You can stay in here, Em won't mind," he told me. "I'll be downstairs if you need anything."

"Who's Em?" I asked.

"President's daughter," he answered, and his voice held a hint of something. Not sadness, but . . . *something.* "She's a little older than you, about my age. Get some rest."

I waited until I heard his footsteps going down the stairs before I pulled off my jeans and climbed into the bed. My head really was hurting now, and while they'd given me pain meds at the hospital, I wouldn't be able to take another dose for a while longer. Lying there, I stared at the ceiling, wondering what Painter was doing downstairs.

Did he have a girlfriend?

Right, like it even mattered. He'd been sweet to me, but he was probably sweet to little old ladies, too. Guys like that didn't go for girls like me.

Girls who were nothing.

The thought hurt, but eventually I drifted off. When I woke it was nearly five. Wandering downstairs, I found Loni and Reese sitting in the living room, her perched on his lap as they talked quietly.

"Sorry, I didn't mean to interrupt you," I said, feeling like an intruder.

"Don't worry about it," Reese replied, sounding resigned. Loni pushed off him, then came over to study me carefully. She was shorter than I was, and I felt awkward and gawky next to her.

"How are you feeling?" she asked, her eyes sharp.

"Good, my head hardly hurts at all," I said, and this time it was the truth. "Although I'm starving."

Then I snapped my mouth shut, because it sounded like I was begging for food, which I guess I was. I mean, I was sort of trapped here, out in the country at a strange house owned by a man I didn't even know, and whose only tie to me was that he was sleeping with my best friend's aunt.

That's pretty damned tenuous.

Loni smiled. "If you're hungry, that means you're healthy. I picked up some new clothes for you earlier. They're in the bag."

She pointed to a Target bag sitting on the floor next to the stairwell. I'd just leaned over to grab it when Painter walked into the room from the back of the house.

"How you doin'?" he asked.

"Better," I managed to reply, feeling shy.

"Get changed and we'll go out to dinner," Reese announced. "It's been a long day."

"Okay," I said gratefully, then ran upstairs to put on my new clothes. Hopefully Loni had gotten me something cute.

***

Painter invited himself along with us, which pissed Loni off for reasons I couldn't quite understand. I knew she was protective, but it wasn't like he was doing anything.

Sure, he'd insisted that I ride with him to the restaurant (which kicked ass, I might add). And he was sitting next to me in the booth, his thick, male thigh pressed up against the side of mine, which gave me little flutters and chills. A couple times he leaned over to ask if my food was all right, and when we finished he draped his arm across the back of the booth, right behind my head.

I'd sat there, wanting him so bad it took everything I had not to shiver. I'd have given anything to kiss him. At one point he even reached down and gave my knee another of those little squeezes, nearly giving me a heart attack.

Loni glared at him throughout.

Reese rolled his eyes and ordered another beer.

Afterward, Painter gave me a ride back to Reese's house, and I swear if he'd asked me, I would've done anything for him. To him. But he didn't . . . Nope, he just dropped me off.

But as I got off his bike, he tucked a strand of my hair back behind my ear and skimmed his fingers across my cheekbone. I really did shiver then, because how could I not?

***

Two days later I was bored out of my mind.

I'd found myself in a weird limbo out at the Hayes house, because I had no transportation or way to get to work. There wasn't anyone to talk to, either—Reese and Loni were gone most of the time, her working and him doing club stuff. There had been some big party the night before, but yours truly wasn't invited.

Instead I just sat around, waiting for something to happen. Reese still made me nervous, but I trusted London and it wasn't like I had any other options. Even the money I'd managed to hide from my dad was gone, burned up in the explosion. Now all I had were the clothes Loni had given me.

Two pairs of panties. One bra. A pair of shorts and a pair of jeans, two tank tops and a sweatshirt.

That was it—the sum total of all my worldly possessions.

I needed to take action, figure things out . . . But when I tried to talk to Loni and Reese about the next step, neither of them had time for me. Loni had work stuff, Reese had club stuff, and they both just kept telling me to rest up and let my head heal.

A girl can only rest so much, though.

That's why I was just sitting on the porch Saturday afternoon, trying to read when I heard the bikes coming. Now, if I'd learned anything over the past two days, I'd learned that there were always bikes coming and going from Reese Hayes' house, so I didn't think too much of it when I saw the motorcycles turn into the driveway. Then I recognized one of the riders as Painter, and my heart clenched. (Okay, so it wasn't my heart that clenched, it was something centered a lot lower in my body, but don't judge me. Painter was the kind of hot that no sane woman can resist. It never occurred to me to try.)

"Hi," I managed to say as he swaggered toward the porch—and yeah, he had the swagger down cold, trust me.

"Hey," he replied, giving me that same slow grin that'd first melted me at the hospital. (And the house. And the restaurant . . .) "This is Puck. Me and him are gonna hang out here tonight."

I shot a look at his friend, who was a tall, solidly built guy with darkish skin, darker hair and a nasty scar across his face. He didn't look much older than me, but the flatness of his eyes sort of freaked me out.

"Reese didn't say anything about someone coming over," I replied, torn. I wanted Painter around, but his friend? Not so much. "I should probably check with Loni."

"Feel free," Puck said. "But we got orders. President says we're watching the house and keeping an eye on you, so that's what we're doing."

Painter scowled at him. "Way to scare her, fuckwad."

Puck didn't say anything, just crossed his arms over his chest, making it clear he was here to stay. Okay. This was getting weird fast.

"You know, why don't you just come in?" I said quickly. I hated it when people fought. Mom and Dad fought all the time, at least until she stopped giving a shit and started smoking pot constantly. "I think there's some pork chops in the fridge. I'll make them for dinner, does that sound good?"

Painter smiled at me again, and this time there was something strained about the expression. "Sounds perfect, babe. Can't wait."

***

Dinner was weird. For one thing, we didn't talk. None of us. We just sat and ate in the same room together, the clicking of our knives and forks almost painfully loud. Painter was nothing like he'd been before . . . He was still nice to me, but distant. No little knee touches, no lingering glances.

Nothing whispered in my ear.

The situation with Puck was strange, too. I'd assumed they were friends, but soon realized they hardly knew each other. Not that it mattered—they'd been sent to the house with orders to watch over me, and that's what they planned to do. This burst my bubble in a big way, because I'd been secretly hoping that Painter had wanted to see me again. In reality, I was an assignment. I didn't know why Reese thought I needed a babysitter, but he obviously did.

I'd just finished my pork chop when Painter suggested we watch a movie.

"It'll help pass the time," Puck agreed, anything but friendly. "I'll see what's available. Good food—thanks."

He stood and carried his plate into the kitchen, then passed by us again on his way to the living room. Painter leaned back in his own seat, looking me over.

"How are you doing?" he asked, and it sounded like he was actually interested in the answer. I shrugged.

"Good," I said. "Although it's a little weird . . . I don't feel safe going home. Loni's place is gone. I'm not quite sure what I'm still doing out here, but I don't have anywhere else to go, either. I can't even get to my job, because I don't have a car. Loni and Reese are never here. It's hard to wrap my head around what comes next, you know?"

Huh. That was a *lot* more than I'd planned on sharing. I stared down at my plate, wondering if I sounded like a whiny little girl. Painter didn't respond, so I shot him a look under my lashes. He was studying me intently, although I couldn't read his expression.

"Wish I had an answer for you," he finally said. "It's a fucked up situation and I got no idea what happens next."

That caught me off guard, because it was so honest. Whenever I managed to corner Loni, she'd just tell me that everything would be okay, and that she'd take care of me. Reese said to calm down, that it would all work out.

Hearing the truth was scary, but refreshing, too.

"Thanks," I blurted out.

"For what?" he asked.

"For being honest. Everyone is telling me that things are fine, but they aren't. I've got no home, no family to help me, no transportation and if I don't find a way to get to work soon, I'll lose my job. Not that I'd even *know* if I got fired, because my phone blew up with the rest of the house. And I've probably got a bazillion dollars in medical bills, too. It *is* a fucked up situation, so why is everyone pretending it's not?"

He seemed startled by my sudden burst of speech, which I could understand. I'd startled me, too.

"You know, the house probably wasn't your fault," he said slowly. I shook my head, wishing it was true.

"I think I left the gas burner turned on after I made my macaroni and cheese," I admitted. "What else could've caused it?"

"Melanie, leaving on a burner for a couple hours doesn't blow up a house," he told me, the words gentle. "I mean, it's not something you want to go around doing, but whatever happened, it was because of something bigger than you cooking macaroni. It's not your fault. And Loni's insurance will probably cover your medical bills, too."

"I really hope that's true about the house," I said, although I knew in my gut it wasn't. I'd caught a whiff of gas earlier that evening and had meant to investigate. Instead I'd gotten distracted thinking about my mom. "And I guess the medical bills don't really matter anyway. Not like they can collect."

He nodded, reaching for the beer he'd grabbed from the fridge earlier. Taking a long drink, he glanced toward the living room, where I could hear Puck rummaging around.

"You don't have to watch a movie with us if you don't want to," he said quietly. "You can go upstairs and rest."

"I'll watch it," I insisted, and not just because I wanted to spend more time with him. I'd had my fill of rest over the past two days. Just having another human being around to talk to was a relief—the fact that he was a super sexy human made it that much better. "Here, let me get your plate."

"No, that's all right, I'll take it," he said, so we carried the dishes into the kitchen together. He stood and watched while I loaded the dishwasher. Every time I passed him, I caught his scent. Leather and something strange . . . like paint thinner.

"Is Painter your real name?" I asked, avoiding his eyes.

"Nope, my real name is Levi Brooks," he said. "But I like to paint, and most guys in the club use a road name, so there you have it."

"Like, paint houses?"

He laughed. "No, pictures. I'm into art."

That surprised me. It must've shown on my face, because he gave another low chuckle. "Let me guess, you assumed bikers aren't sophisticated enough to appreciate art?"

I coughed, looking away. I'd be damned if I'd answer.

"You're cute when you blush," he said, reaching over to catch a lock of my hair, tugging on it gently. *He called me cute!* My heart stopped for an instant, and it was hard to follow the rest of his words. "And yeah, I like art. I do a lot of the custom work down at the body shop. All the gold on my Harley is my own, too. Sometimes I do bigger projects. Usually painting on boards for customers who want portraits of their bikes, believe it or not."

"Wow," I said. God, he was so out of my league—hot *and* talented.

"What about you?" he asked. "What do you do?"

"Well, right now I'm waiting tables," I told him, wishing I had a more interesting job. "But I'm starting school in the fall, at North Idaho College. And once I get all my prerequisites done, I'm going to study nursing. I like taking care of people."

"Yeah, I can see that. You're friends with Jessica, right? London's niece?"

I nodded.

"You take care of her a lot?" I shrugged, because I took care of her all the time, but he didn't need to know that. At least, I'd taken care of her until she'd run off to California to live with her mom. She'd been super pissed at London for dragging her out of a party at the Reapers clubhouse, which was my fault in a way.

I was the one who ratted her out.

I'd heard a lot of rumors about those parties, about how wild they were. How a girl could get into trouble. Looking at Painter, I believed those rumors, too—if he crooked his finger at me, I'd come running like a shot.

The thought caught me off guard, and I frowned. Since when did I come running for a guy?

"You okay?" Painter asked.

"Sure," I said, although I was feeling more than a little off balance. Not physically, but mentally, because in the past two days I'd gone from being afraid of bikers to really, really liking this particular one.

How many girls did he have waiting for him, back at that clubhouse of his?

I looked up to find him staring at me, his face thoughtful.

"Let's go see what Puck found for movies," he said. "And Mel?"

"Yeah?"

"Things aren't okay, but they will be. You can get through this."

"Thanks," I whispered, and to my disgust I felt hot tears filling my eyes. I hated crying, hated the kind of girls who cried. Hated looking and feeling weak, but Painter just pulled me into his arms, holding me tight as sobs started shaking my body.

I missed my mom really bad, and I was scared.

He rubbed my back, whispering softly into my ear, although I had no idea what he was saying. All I knew was that for the first time in forever—maybe years—I felt safe.

***

An hour later, that whole "safe" thing had passed.

I was sitting in the living room, huddled in a blanket on the couch as I watched a scarred and twisted man carrying a chain saw creep up behind an innocent young woman.

He was going to kill her.

I knew this because I'd already watched him kill at least ten other people with his horrible weapon, and the movie wasn't even halfway over yet.

Why the hell hadn't I gone upstairs when I had a chance?

Now I couldn't, of course. Not alone in the darkness of the stairwell—not even if I turned on every light in the damned place. My mind could tell me there wasn't anyone lying in wait to murder me all it wanted, but my gut knew better—the instant I stuck my feet outside the blanket, they'd get cut off.

This sucked, because I really had to pee.

"You okay?" Painter murmured, leaning down close to me. I jumped, startled, and then he was wrapping his arm around my shoulders, pulling me closer to him. The saw roared through the sound system, and I closed my eyes tight as the girl started screaming and screaming. Painter's hand rubbed my shoulder, and he gave me a squeeze. "You want us to turn it off?"

Shaking my head, I burrowed into the warmth of his body. The saw roared again and I moaned.

"Seriously, we can turn it off," he whispered, close enough to the side of my face that I could feel the heat of his breath, and smell the faintest hint of beer.

"I'm fine," I insisted, wondering if I'd ever sleep again. I hated horror movies. *Hated* them. Jessica made fun of me for it all the time, but I'd be damned if I'd admit how scared I was. Not to Painter.

"Okay, then," he said, and I felt something brush my hair. His hand?

"Good news," Puck announced, sounding almost cheerful. He was sitting in a chair across the room, watching us with something like humor in his eyes. "This is a whole series. We can do a marathon."

I moaned again, wondering if I could just roll up into a ball and die, right here.

It would be better than spending the night watching blood spurt. Would it ever end?

***

I woke up in bed, fully clothed under the bedding.

Staring at the ceiling, I blinked, trying to figure out how I'd gotten here. There had been the never-ending, hateful movie marathon. Painter holding me, which was significantly less hateful. London coming home, talking to him in the kitchen and then locking herself in the bedroom.

Had I fallen asleep next to Painter on the couch?

Maybe he carried me upstairs, tucked me in. God, how sexy was that?

Not as sexy as him crawling into bed next to you . . .

A wave of heat spread through me. What would it feel like to sleep with him? Or maybe we wouldn't sleep at all, just spend the night—

Stop it, I told myself firmly. *Stop it right now. If he wanted to make a move, he could've. He didn't. Get over yourself, already.*

***

"Mel, how much longer until I can put you on the schedule again?" asked Kirstie, sounding impatient. She was my manager at the restaurant and I was talking to her on my new phone. She'd been horrified to hear about the explosion and so far hadn't complained about all the time off, but that wouldn't last forever. Either I needed to move somewhere I could walk to work, or I needed a car.

At least I could make calls again.

The phone was a gift from Reese. He'd tossed it casually across the table at me over breakfast on Sunday morning, not long after I'd dragged my chainsaw-traumatized ass downstairs. Puck was sitting at the breakfast table, and I looked around, hoping to see Painter.

No such luck.

After we finished eating, I tried to pin Loni down again, but she didn't want to talk. Neither did Reese. Everyone just seemed to think I should sit quietly in the corner and stay out of their way—but how was I supposed to rebuild my life stuck in a corner?

There was a reality disconnect here, and it felt like I was the only person who could see it.

I spent Sunday sulking, and by Monday—yet another day alone in the house—I was on the edge of losing it. London came home in the late afternoon and started fixing dinner, even more distracted and out of focus than she'd been before. I tried to help her, but I just kept getting in her way so eventually I went upstairs.

By myself.

Again.

I was laying on the bed, reading an old science fiction book I'd found in the closet. It wasn't really my thing, but seeing as this was my fourth straight day of doing jack shit, I'd decided to expand my horizons.

A crisp knock came at the door.

"It's open," I called, and looked up, expecting to see Loni. Instead I found Painter. He gave me that super sexy smile of his, walking toward the bed with long, loose strides. Then he sat down next to me, and I swear to God, my heartbeat doubled.

"Hey, Mel," he said, reaching over to slowly pull the book out of my hands. "You want to go out for a while tonight?"

"Like, on a date?" I gasped, then could've smacked myself, because how desperate was that? Painter didn't seem bothered, though.

"Yeah, a date," he said, sounding bemused. "I thought we'd get dinner, maybe go see a movie."

That sounded amazing, unreal . . . except for the movie part. I couldn't do it again, I realized. Not even with his arms around me. "No horror," I said, hoping it wasn't a deal breaker. Painter grinned.

"How about this, I'll let you pick," he replied. "I want you to have fun. You ready?"

I thought about my hair, which hadn't been combed all day.

Maybe my clothes weren't great and I didn't have any makeup, but I still wanted to primp a little before we left. Hell, what I really needed was a moment alone to catch my breath.

Levi "Painter" Brooks was taking me on a date!

"Give me five minutes," I told him. "Then I'll be ready to go."

"Sounds great," he said, standing up again. Then he reached down, offering me his hand. I took it, and he pulled me up and into him. We stood there for an instant—touching—before he stepped back.

"Sorry about that," he said, but he didn't really sound sorry. I tried to keep it casual as he turned away, leaving me alone to get ready. It was almost impossible. I wanted to jump and dance and scream like a little girl. That's how excited I was.

Instead I splashed some cold water on my face and brushed my hair, wishing I could do more to pretty myself up. Unfortunately, the options were limited.

It would have to be good enough.

***

He took me to a bar and grill in midtown, and to my surprise they didn't bother carding me when he ordered a beer for each of us. I guess when your date is a six-foot-plus biker who's simultaneously badass and beautiful, the average waitress isn't paying attention to anyone's age.

The first sip was bitter, nothing like the Bud Light kegs at our high school parties. I sucked it down, though, and by the time our pizza arrived I had a nice buzz going. Obviously it was a lot stronger than Bud Light, too.

"I really need to find a place in town, so I can walk to work," I told him, trying not to gross him out while I ate. The pizza here was good. Really good. They'd brought it hot from the oven, and there was melted cheese running all over the place. It tasted amazing, but it didn't lend itself to delicate eating.

"Either that or a car," he said, nodding his head. "I'll talk to the prez—maybe he has something you can borrow."

"Do you have any idea what their plan is?" I asked him. "Loni and Reese, I mean. They're still not talking to me, but I'm done sitting around like a potted plant. Tomorrow I'm going to work even if I have to walk."

A strange look crossed Painter's face, and he sighed. "You can borrow my car."

I sat back, stunned.

"I wasn't trying to beg," I told him, suddenly uncomfortable.

"Look, I'm not using it much anyway," he replied. "It's summer—I'd rather ride my bike. I'm heading out of town for a couple days, but I'll have one of the prospects bring it over, drop it off for you. That way you can start working again, get back on your feet."

I didn't know what to say.

"That might be the nicest thing anyone's ever done for me," I whispered. Painter's smile grew strained, and something dark flickered through his eyes.

"Don't thank me too much," he said. He looked away, waving toward the waitress. She hustled her ass right over, and I couldn't blame her. I'd be hustling too, if he was sitting at one of my tables. "Can I get the check?"

"Sure," she cooed at him. I watched as she leaned over, flashing her cleavage. He wasn't looking at her, though.

He was looking at me.

"I'm sorry," he said quietly.

"Sorry for what?"

The waitress came back, handing over our check. Painter pulled out his wallet and grabbed several bills, stuffing them in the little black folder. Then he was on his feet and it was time to go.

He never told me what he was sorry for.

***

I picked an action movie.

There was a romantic comedy that looked good, but after he offered to loan me his car that just seemed cruel. He bought the tickets and we started toward the theater. We were almost inside when he paused to check his phone. Then his face turned grim.

"What's up?" I asked.

"Nothing," he said shortly. That was a lie if I'd ever heard one.

"No, something's wrong. Do you need to go?"

He hesitated, and I knew he did.

"We should go," I said firmly. "You can take me home, and then deal with whatever that was." I nodded toward the phone.

"Yeah, we might want to do that," he admitted. "I'm sorry—I didn't mean to cut things short."

"It's fine. I've had a great time. I'm just sorry the tickets are wasted."

"No worries," he replied. "C'mon."

The ride back was different. I'd lost the sense of breathless expectation that'd filled me earlier in the evening. Painter's body was tense. Whatever message he'd gotten, it wasn't good. We pulled up to Reese's house to find it dark. I stepped off the bike and looked around, startled to see that Reese's motorcycle was gone, along with London's van.

"Where is everyone?"

"Let's go inside," Painter said, dodging my question. I followed him in, then turned, looking at him expectantly for an explanation. Something was up, this was obvious. He knew what it was, too.

"Well?" I asked when he didn't answer my question.

"Reese and Loni are leaving town," he said. "Most of the club is going with them. We've got some business to deal with in Portland. You can just stay here for now, okay? I'll have the prospects bring my car over for you in the morning."

He reached down and pulled out his wallet, opening it and counting out a stack of cash. "You can use this to get a place if . . . Well, if things don't work out here."

I stared at the money blankly—those were hundred dollar bills. "I can't take that."

He reached for his phone, checked it again. "I don't have time to argue with you. Take the fucking money."

With that, he grabbed my hand, wrapping it around the bills. Then he started toward the door, something almost angry about the way he moved.

"Painter," I called after him, confused.

He turned back to me. "You can do it, Mel."

"What?"

"You can make it through this. Whatever happens, don't forget that."

"Painter, what the hell is going on?" I demanded. There was a seriously bad feeling in the pit of my stomach. He shook his head, taking a step toward me. Suddenly his hands were in my hair, jerking me into his body as his lips touched mine.

It wasn't a movie kiss.

He didn't stick his tongue in, and it hurt more than anything. Just a mashing of our lips together like he couldn't help himself, until he shoved me away.

"Go to bed," he growled, wiping off his mouth with the back of his hand, like I disgusted him. Something painful twisted inside.

"Why?"

"Just go to fucking bed, Melanie. Tomorrow you can take the car and you can start looking for a place."

Then he turned away and walked out the door.

***

The next morning I woke up to find a dark blue Toyota SUV in the driveway and a set of keys on the dining room table. I drove it to work, and after my shift I went to the library so I could use the internet.

I needed to find an apartment.

That was Tuesday.

On Wednesday I sat alone on the porch, wondering if anyone would ever come back. By Thursday I'd given up on them. Loni was gone, just like my mom, and she'd taken Painter with her. I worked a double shift, and talked to one of my fellow waitresses about a bedroom in the house she rented with friends.

She thought one of them might be moving out in a couple weeks.

Friday morning, I woke to the sound of a big diesel truck in the driveway. Rushing downstairs, I opened the front door to see London climbing down from the vehicle, looking exhausted. Reese was already out, and then another person slid out of the crew cab. My best friend, Jessica—the same girl who'd thrown a tantrum and run off to California not long ago. Her hand was bandaged and strapped to her body in a sling. Bruises covered her face.

There was no sign of Painter.

Reese walked over to me slowly, glancing at the SUV parked in the driveway.

"He said you can borrow it as long as you want," he said bluntly.

"Why isn't he with you?" I asked, but I could already see the answer written across his face. Something had happened. Something bad.

"He's in jail," Reese said. "And I think he'll be there for a while longer. He said to tell you he's sorry."

"For what?"

"I don't know. Maybe you should write and ask him."

The End

MELANIE AND PAINTER'S STORY CONTINUES IN:

REAPER'S FALL

He never meant to hurt her.

Levi "Painter" Brooks was nothing before he joined the Reapers motorcycle club. The day he patched in, they became his brothers and his life. All they asked in return was a strong arm and unconditional loyalty—a loyalty that's tested when he's caught and sentenced to prison for a crime committed on their behalf.

Melanie Tucker may have had a rough start, but along the way she's learned to fight for her future. She's escaped from hell and started a new life, yet every night she dreams of a biker whose touch she can't forget. It all started out so innocently—just a series of letters to a lonely man in prison. Friendly. Harmless. Safe.

Now Painter Brooks is coming home… and Melanie's about to learn that there's no room for innocence in the Reapers MC.

ALSO FROM JOANNA WYLDE

AUTHOR'S NOTE: *All the Reapers and Silver Bastards MC books stand alone, and can be read in any order.*

REAPER'S PROPERTY

Marie doesn't need a complication like Horse. The massive, tattooed, badass biker who shows up at her brother's house one afternoon doesn't agree. He wants Marie on his bike and in his bed. Now.

But Marie just left her abusive jerk of an ex-husband and she's not looking for a new man. Especially one like Horse—she doesn't know his real name or where he lives, she's ninety percent certain he's a criminal and that the "business" he talks with her brother isn't website design. She needs him out of her life, which would be a snap if he'd just stop giving her mind-blowing orgasms.

Horse is part of the Reapers Motorcycle Club, and when he wants something, he takes it. What he wants is Marie, but she's not interested in becoming "property of".

Then her brother steals from the club. Marie can save him by giving Horse what he wants—at home, in public, on his bike... If she's a very, very good girl, he'll let her brother live.

Maybe.

REAPER'S LEGACY

Eight years ago, Sophie gave her heart—and her virginity—to Zach Barrett on a night that couldn't have been less romantic or more embarrassing. Zach's step-brother, a steely-muscled, tattooed biker named Ruger, caught them in the act, getting a peep show of Sophie he's never forgotten.

She may have lost her dignity that fateful night, but Sophie also gained something precious—her son Noah. Unfortunately, Zach's a deadbeat dad, leaving Ruger to be Noah's only male role model. When he discovers Sophie and his nephew living in near poverty, Ruger takes matters into his own hands—with the help of the Reapers Motorcycle Club—to give them a better life.

Living with outlaw bikers wasn't Sophie's plan for her son, but Ruger isn't giving her a choice. He'll be there for Noah, whether she wants him or not. But Sophie *does* want him, has always wanted him. Now she'll learn that taking a biker to bed can get a girl dirty in every way...

DEVIL'S GAME

Liam "Hunter" Blake hates the Reapers MC. Born and raised a Devil's Jack, he knows his duty. He'll defend his club from their oldest enemies—the Reapers—using whatever weapons he can find. But why use force when the Reapers' president has a daughter who's alone and vulnerable? Hunter has wanted her from the minute he saw her, and now he has an excuse to take her.

Em has lived her entire life in the shadow of the Reapers. Her overprotective father, Picnic, is the club's president. The last time she had a boyfriend, Picnic shot him. Now the men in her life are far more interested in keeping her daddy happy than showing her a good time. Then she meets a handsome stranger—a man who isn't afraid to treat her like a real woman. One who isn't afraid of her father. His name is Liam, and he's The One.

Or so she thinks.

REAPER'S STAND

As Reapers Motorcycle Club president, Reese "Picnic" Hayes has given his entire life to the club. After losing his wife, he knew he'd never love another woman. And with two daughters to raise and a club to manage, that was just fine with him. These days, Reese keeps his relationships free and easy—he definitely doesn't want to waste his time on a glorified cleaning lady like London Armstrong.

Too bad he's completely obsessed with her.

Besides running her own business, London's got her junkie cousin's daughter to look after—a more reckless than average eighteen-year-old. Sure she's attracted to the Reapers' president, but she's not stupid. Reese Hayes is a criminal and a thug. But when her young cousin gets caught up with a ruthless drug cartel, Reese might be the only man who can help her. Now London has to make the hardest decision of her life—how far will she go to save her family?

REAPERS FALL

Levi "Painter" Brooks was nothing before he joined the Reapers motorcycle club. The day he patched in, they became his brothers and his life. All they asked in return was a strong arm and unconditional loyalty—a loyalty that's tested when he's caught and sentenced to prison for a crime committed on their behalf.

Melanie Tucker may have had a rough start, but along the way she's learned to fight for her future. She's escaped from hell and started a new life, yet every night she dreams of a biker whose touch she can't forget. It all started out so innocently—just a series of letters to a lonely man in prison. Friendly. Harmless. Safe.

Now Painter Brooks is coming home… and Melanie's about to learn that there's no room for innocence in the Reapers MC.

SILVER BASTARD

First in the new Silver Valley series.

Fourteen months. For fourteen months, Puck Redhouse sat in a cell and kept his mouth shut, protecting the Silver Bastards MC from their enemies. Then he was free and it was time for his reward—full membership in the club, along with a party to celebrate. That's when he saw Becca Jones for the first time and set everything in motion. Before the night ended he'd violated his parole and stolen her away from everything she knew.

Five years. It was five years ago that Puck destroyed Becca and saved her all in one night. She's been terrified of him ever since, but she's even more terrified of the monsters he still protects her from . . . But Becca refuses to let fear control her. She's living her life and moving forward, until she gets a phone call from the past she can't ignore. She has to go back, and there's only one man she can trust to go with her—the ex-con biker who rescued her once before.

Puck will help her again, but this time it'll be on his terms. No more lies, no more tears, and no more holding back what he really wants . . .

Made in United States
Troutdale, OR
01/26/2024